THE RANCHER'S DAUGHTER

ELIZABETH KELLY

EK PUBLISHING INC.

THE RANCHER'S DAUGHTER

He's all she's ever wanted.

Confident and curvy, all Evelyn Crawford is looking for is a night of fun with no strings attached. The last person she expects to see at the bar is the man she's been in love with for most of her life.

All Thomas Sinclair wants is a quiet night and a cold beer. What he doesn't expect to see is Evelyn in an outfit that reveals every tempting curve. He's made a promise to Evelyn's father to protect her from men like him, but this night changes everything. His resolve to keep his distance is tested by Evelyn's determination to show him exactly what he's been missing.

CHAPTER 1

He didn't recognize her at first. He had checked her out, of course, just like every other man in the bar had. She was hard to miss in that tight, short skirt. The combination of her heels and skirt made her legs look impossibly long.

She obviously was not used to heels. Even he could see how she wobbled a little on them as she shifted from foot to foot and nervously tossed her long blonde hair. It made her cute in an awkward, newborn colt kind of way, and if there hadn't been a cluster of men already standing around her, he would have considered buying her a drink.

He sat back in the booth and took a drink of beer, studying the way the skirt clung to her ass. She was curvy in all the right places. He smiled a little. He liked curvy. Always had and always would. There was something about a full ass, large breasts, and a nice round tummy that made his blood hot.

He took another sip of beer. He knew exactly where the attraction came from. His childhood babysitter and his first crush was a girl named Betty. She carried an extra forty pounds on her small frame, and she was soft and sweet with large breasts and wide hips. He'd loved her fiercely, and his ten-year-old heart was broken when her family moved away.

He finished his beer, briefly considered muscling his way in beside the other three men standing in front of her, and then stood and jammed his cowboy hat on his head. He would be better off to head home. Tomorrow would be a long day, and a man pushing forty was too old to pick up women at the bar.

He crossed the crowded bar and took one final look at the blonde's ass before heading toward the door. One of the men beside her said something, and she laughed - a low and husky sound that he immediately recognized. The hair on the back of his neck stood up, and he twisted around to stare at the woman. It couldn't be - there was no way it was her. She didn't go to bars, and even if she did, she certainly wouldn't dress like that.

She laughed again, and his feet propelled him forward before his brain fully comprehended what he was doing. He grabbed the woman's arm, not failing to notice the firmness of her arm under her shirt, and spun her around.

"Hey! What the hell -"

She squeaked to a stop and stared up at him in shock. "What are you doing here, Thomas?"

He couldn't speak - hell, he couldn't breathe. She wore a loose shirt, unbuttoned nearly to her navel. Under it, she wore a white bustier. The white material contrasted sharply with her tanned skin. He couldn't stop staring at the way the bustier hugged her large breasts like a lover's touch. Her breasts strained at the material, the tops of them barely covered by the bustier, and he wondered how long it would take before they simply busted free of the overstressed fabric.

"Thomas!" The woman said sharply. He dragged his eyes away from her exquisite breasts and up to her face.

"What am I doing here? What are you doing here, Evelyn? Does your father know you're here?"

"I'm twenty-eight years old, Thomas. I don't need my father's permission to go to a bar." She tugged at his hand. "Let go of me, please."

"No. I'm taking you home."

"Like hell you are," she said with a light whack on his broad chest.

He scowled at her. "This place is nothing but a meat market. I'm taking you home."

She snatched her arm free and teetered on her high heels. She would have fallen if he hadn't reached out and snagged her arm again.

"I'm not a child, Thomas. Stop treating me like one."

His eyes shifted to her breasts again. They rose and fell rapidly with her anger, and his dick stirred in his pants. Jesus, she definitely wasn't a child.

"Evelyn, you -"

"What gives you the right to tell me what to do?" she said before glancing over her shoulder at the men behind them.

"I'm your stepbrother," he said grimly.

"Ex-stepbrother. My dad divorced your mom three wives ago."

One of the men stepped forward and placed a meaty hand on Evelyn's shoulder. "Is there a problem?"

"No, not at all." Evelyn smiled sweetly at him. "Just give me a minute."

"Take your hand off her," Thomas growled at the man.

The man frowned but didn't move his hand. "The lady and I were just about to dance. I suggest you remove *your* hand, friend."

Thomas stared steadily at the man. He was tall like Thomas. Although at 6'3", Thomas still had the height advantage, and he could tell the man was soft. He could see it in the man's manicured hand, in the expensive shirt he wore, and in the way his belly protruded over his belt.

"You would be wise, *friend*," Thomas said with a cool glance at the man, "to walk away."

The man hesitated and then removed his hand from Evelyn's shoulder before slowly walking away.

"Thank you so much, Thomas." Evelyn scowled at him. "God, you're such an ass."

Ignoring her insult, he said, "Let's go, Evelyn," and then grunted with frustration when she yanked her arm free of his grip again.

"No. I came here to dance, and I'm going to dance." She turned, wobbling like crazy on her heels, and yelped in surprise when he took her upper arm and steered her towards the dance floor. "What are you doing?"

"You want to dance? Fine, we'll dance one dance, and then I'm taking you home. No arguments, Evelyn."

Thomas nearly pushed her onto the smooth dance floor as the band finished playing, and the people on the dance floor whooped and clapped. They stood in awkward silence until the band started up the next song.

"This next one is for all the lovers out there." The lead singer grinned into the microphone as they played a slow song.

Thomas hesitated before putting his arm around Evelyn's waist and pulling her against him. He took her right hand in his left and moved her around the small dance floor.

"Thomas, this is ridiculous. I don't want to dance with you." She pounded him on his back with her left hand.

He winced a little. It wasn't surprising how strong she was. Hell, he'd seen her lift sixty-five-pound bales of hay easily. She was a ranch kid. She might be curvy, but she also had muscles from years of outdoor work.

"Too bad," he said. He dragged Evelyn closer until her

body pressed tightly against his and clamped his hand firmly around her hip. "One dance, and then I'm taking you home. I don't care if I have to throw you over my shoulder and carry you out of here kicking and screaming. Do you get it, Evelyn?"

She snorted in defeat. "Yeah, I get it."

"Good. Maybe you should tell me just what the hell you're doing here. This is no place for a -"

"Maybe *you* could shut it for a minute, Thomas. What do you say? If this will be my only dance of the night, then I'd like to close my eyes and pretend you're someone else. Your yapping is ruining the effect," she said.

"Fine," he huffed.

He held her a little tighter and steered her around the dance floor. He took a deep breath. She smelled like violets. He'd never noticed her scent before. Did she always smell like violets? He'd worked beside her for years, baling hay, milking cows, and riding horses, and he had never once noticed her scent. Maybe it was because he had never allowed himself to be this close to her before.

He couldn't say that he'd never noticed her body. He was a guy, after all. But she wore jeans and loose t-shirts when working the ranch. He had checked her ass out a time or two, and her breasts weren't completely hidden under the loose t-shirts, but he'd always felt guilty about it.

In the last few years, though, he'd found it increasingly difficult not to wonder if her skin was as soft as it looked, not to imagine what it would sound like to have her low voice moaning his name, and not to picture how good she would look naked in his bed. He used to have some control over his thoughts, and now he was a goddamn pervert.

Forgetting that she was ten years younger than him, she was his stepsister. It may have only been for a year, and maybe it'd been twenty years ago, but it didn't change the fact that for a brief time, their parents were married. He used to find it easy to keep his eyes to himself when it came to her.

Well, most of the time, anyway. There had been that one time when Evelyn was eighteen and had come to the guest-house. She would never know how difficult it was to send her back to her house. Thank God she left the ranch for college soon after that. When she returned four years later, he had almost forgotten how she looked that night.

Of course, he thought grimly, the white bustier did a fine job of reminding him. Sweat broke out on his forehead, and he grimaced and moved his pelvis away from hers. Jesus, he was not about to get an erection while dancing with Evelyn. He stared down at the floor. It was a mistake. He could see the luscious curve of her ass in her indecently tight skirt, not to mention her long legs clad in black nylon. He wondered if she was wearing stockings and if her panties were a thong. The must be. There was no sign of a panty line.

Maybe she's not wearing any panties at all.

His hand tightened on her hip, and he pressed her against him as he fought to keep from moving his hand to her ass and finding out for himself the state of her underwear.

He realized two things an instant too late. One – his efforts to not have an erection had failed miserably, and two – Evelyn's soft gasp clearly indicated that she was well aware of what the hardness was pushing against her hip.

* * *

EVELYN CLOSED HER EYES AND WISHED SHE COULD SUBTLY remove her hand from Thomas' grip and wipe it on her skirt. Her palms were sweating, hell, her entire body was sweating, and she prayed he didn't notice.

She had been lying when she said she didn't want to dance with him and when she told him to be quiet so she could pretend he was someone else. She'd had a crush on Thomas since she was eight years old. Being in his arms, being held against his broad chest with his large, hot hand gripping her hip, had given her that heady thrill she remembered from her youth.

She was devastated when her father divorced Thomas's mother after only a year. She was used to the numerous women that paraded through her house - her father was a notorious ladies' man - but unlike the other women her father dated, Thomas's mother had always been kind to her. Maybe it was because she had a child, or maybe she felt sorry for Evelyn, but Linda was the mother Evelyn so desperately wanted for that short year of marriage.

It wasn't just the loss of Linda. Evelyn couldn't kid herself about that. She'd thrown a fit when her father had announced his intention to divorce Linda, and her reaction completely baffled him. She refused to tell him why she was so upset. There was no way she was confiding in her strict and emotionally unavailable father that she was in love with her stepbrother. He would have shipped her off to the nuthouse.

She was thrilled when Thomas moved back in with them a year later. By then, Linda had a new husband, and Evelyn had overheard her father telling his new girlfriend that Thomas had been in trouble with the law. Linda was at her wit's end with her child, and not sure what else to do, she asked Evelyn's father to take him in. During her father's brief marriage to Linda, Thomas loved working on the ranch and got along well with her father. Her father had welcomed him back with open arms. Thomas was the son he'd always wanted, and he was happy to teach the young man how to run the ranch.

Her father tried to steer Evelyn away from having anything to do with the ranch. She long suspected that he would leave the ranch to Thomas anyway, and when he actively encouraged her to go to college and get her business degree, it only confirmed her suspicions. She left for college, partly to shut him up but mostly so she could finally live her life. Her father was strict and overprotective of his only child, especially regarding men and dating. She hadn't been allowed to date until she was sixteen, and even then, he sent chaperones on their dates. She'd finally just given up on dating when her father cajoled Thomas into chaperoning one of them. The humiliation was too great.

She was a woman literally tripping over dozens of available men working the ranch, but she might as well have been invisible. Not a single ranch hand went near her. Both her father and Thomas saw to that.

Her father kept no such rules for himself, dating - and occasionally marrying - woman after woman. She often wondered if he was so strict about her dating because he didn't want her to end up like one of the many women who paraded through his life.

Her college years were some of the best of her life. She made new friends, studied hard, partied hard, and lost her virginity to a sweet boy she met in her economics class. She dated a few different men but nothing serious, and after she finished her degree, she returned to the ranch. She'd missed it more than she would admit.

Despite her father's disapproval, she went back to working the ranch. She spent the first few years doing the chores next to Thomas and the hired ranch hands until tired of listening to her father rant about her wasted business degree, she switched to the administrative side of the ranch. Now, she spent most of her time working in the small office, handling daily administrative duties, bookkeeping, and payroll.

She enjoyed it well enough, although sitting at a desk all

day hadn't been that great for her ass. Always a curvy girl, she slowly crept up a few sizes now that she was desk-bound. At first, she dieted and did her best to lose the weight, but she decided it wasn't worth it after a few months. She liked her body just the way it was and was confident that she would have no problem attracting men if she attempted to date.

Of course, that didn't pan out either. It didn't seem to matter to her father that she was twenty-two years old and had lived away from home for the last four years. Returning to the ranch and sleeping in her childhood room convinced him he had the right to tell her who she should and shouldn't date.

They'd had argument after argument about it, and finally, in desperation, she'd gone to Thomas. She'd begged him to speak with her father, but he'd only stared at her with an odd look before telling her that her father was just trying to protect her.

She'd flushed a little, remembering the night shortly after her eighteenth birthday when she had crept to the guest-house that Thomas lived in. She wore a long coat and very little else. She was nervous but determined that Thomas would be her first. He'd kindly but firmly rebuffed her attempted seduction, and she'd fled the guesthouse in humiliation. She left for college soon after that, and when she returned nearly four years later, neither of them ever mentioned that night.

She lived at the ranch until she was twenty-five and then found her own place in town. She missed living at the ranch. She missed waking up before the sun rose and going for a solitary horse ride through the fields that made up her father's land, but she was too old to live under her father's rules. She commuted to the ranch to work daily and spent her evenings in the attic apartment she rented.

Oddly enough, despite having her own place and independence, she still hadn't dated much. She told herself it wasn't because of Thomas, and she was over her crush on him. Sure, she might occasionally notice the way his ass looked in those tight jeans he was always wearing, and yeah, maybe his deep voice sent shivers down her spine, but hell, she was only human.

She sighed as he moved her past a young couple practically glued together. They were kissing, and the man had his hand on the woman's ass. She ignored the twinge in her stomach. She was in the middle of a small dry spell - if you called three years without sex a small dry spell – and she had come to the bar in the hopes of getting laid. It was crude but the truth. She wasn't interested in dating for whatever reason, but it didn't mean she didn't occasionally yearn for a warm body in her bed. A vibrator could not replace a man's warmth or hard body.

She'd called her best friend Alice, who was more than happy to join her for a night out. Alice was married with two little girls but was pumped about being Evelyn's wingman. Evelyn felt like a little girl playing dress-up as she squeezed herself into the bustier and skirt and carefully applied the dark red lipstick to her mouth. She was halfway to the bar when Alice had texted her. Her littlest one, Darla, had come down with the flu, and she had to cancel on Evelyn.

Disappointed, she'd almost turned around and headed back home but decided to strike out alone. She was an adult, and if she wanted to have a night of meaningless sex, she could. Everything was going fine – well, mostly fine. Honestly, none of the men in the bar held much interest to her, and then Thomas showed up. Why he was even in this stupid dive bar in the first place was beyond her.

She inhaled deeply. He smelled good. His aftershave was light and spicy, and she pressed a little closer to him. He had a five o'clock shadow on his strong jaw, and she wondered what it would feel like to have that dark stubble rubbing against her nipples.

Her nipples tightened in response, and she scolded herself fiercely. Thomas had made it perfectly clear he had no interest in her. In fact, she never caught him staring at her breasts like most of the men on the ranch did.

He stared tonight.

She shivered delicately. That was true. He'd stared at her breasts tonight, more than once, and she thought there might have even been a look of hunger in his light green eyes. She briefly considered seducing him and then snorted quietly as he moved his body away from her.

No point in that, you idiot. He can't even stand to have you touching him for one dance. Just get through this dance and go home. You've had enough humiliation for one night. In fact, you really should –

Thomas's hand suddenly gripped her hip, and he pressed his body against hers again. She couldn't stop the small gasp from escaping her throat when she felt the unmistakable hardness against her belly.

Thomas not only had an erection, but he was pressing it against her.

CHAPTER 2

Thomas groaned and tried to back away from Evelyn. She released his hand, but instead of allowing him to escape, she threw both her arms around his shoulders and pressed herself against his erection.

He dropped his hand from her waist as the music ended. "Time to go, Evelyn."

She shook her head as another slow song started. "One more dance, Thomas."

"That's not a good idea," he said.

"I think it's a great idea." She smiled at him and rubbed her lower body against the bulge in his jeans. He inhaled sharply, and his hands gripped her waist.

He could feel the soft swell of her stomach pushing against his erection, and his eyes dropped to her chest. Her skin was tanned from the sun. Well, he stared at the milky-white tops of her breasts, most of her skin was tanned. He had a sudden urge to run his finger across all that delectable, unexpectedly pale skin and then under her lingerie to see if her nipples were hard.

He closed his eyes, his fingers digging into her hips as she swayed with the music.

"Evelyn?" He forced himself to look at her. She was only 5'8" or so, but her heels had brought her almost face-to-face with him. Her eyes were hazel, and he noticed the tiny flecks of gold in the left one for the first time.

"Yes, Thomas?" Her breath was sweet on his lips, her small, straight nose nearly brushing against his.

"I – you look very nice tonight."

"Thank you." She wet her lips with her tongue, smiling with satisfaction when his gaze dropped to her mouth.

"Do you think my skirt is scandalously short?" she asked.

"It's shorter than you normally wear." He couldn't remember the last time he had even seen her in a skirt, let alone one that barely covered her ass.

"Very true," she said with a sugar-sweet smile. "I wasn't sure if I should wear the short skirt. My legs aren't really my best feature – they're too thick – but I figured if they didn't like my legs, they could always look at my breasts. They're definitely my best feature. Wouldn't you agree, Thomas?"

"They're, uh, very nice." He felt like a mouse trapped between a cat's paws.

"Thank you. Although I think the nylons and heels make my legs look pretty good. Do you agree?"

When he didn't reply, she pressed her mouth to his ear and nudged the brim of his cowboy hat up with her nose. "Do you agree, Thomas?"

"Are they stockings?" he asked hoarsely.

This was insanity - total insanity - but he suddenly, desperately needed to know.

"They are." Her breath tickled his ear. "I think stockings and a garter is sexy. Don't you, Thomas?"

"Yes." He slid one hand up her back and pressed her

14

breasts harder against him. "What kind of panties are you wearing?"

"Why don't you find out for yourself?" she said.

He glanced around the dance floor before steering her past the couples swaying and circling in time to the music and toward the far end of the dance space. It was darker and quieter there, and he pressed her against the wall.

He took another quick look around to confirm that no one had noticed them. He slid his hand down Evelyn's leg, squeezing her nylon-clad thigh before slipping it up under her skirt. She made a soft, breathless little moan when he cupped her naked ass. His fingers probed between her ass cheeks, finding the soft and silky material between them. He squeezed her ass again, pushing her against his erection as he breathed into her ear, "A thong."

"You sound disappointed." She let her lips brush against his earlobe.

He stroked the straps of the garter before running his fingers over her stocking. "I was hoping for no panties."

"What kind of girl do you think I am, Thomas?" She pressed her soft lips just below her ear, and he jerked against her.

"I'm beginning to think I have no idea what kind of girl you are," he muttered.

"Of course," her hand drifted down his back, stroking him through his t-shirt, "the no panties thing could easily be done. I could simply slip to the ladies' room and take them off."

He inhaled sharply and ground his pelvis against hers in a heated response. She gave another one of those soft, husky moans that set his skin on fire.

"Or," she said, "we could go to your truck, and you could take my panties off for me."

* * *

WHEN THOMAS DIDN'T REPLY TO HER SUGGESTION, EVELYN worried she'd gone too far. When he turned away from her, she knew she had. Her heart plummeted straight to the damn floor, but he looked over his shoulder at her, his green eyes dark with need, and she felt an answering surge of desire in her belly.

He held his hand out to her. "C'mon."

She took his hand, and he strode quickly across the dance floor, dragging her past the crowds of people and out the door of the bar.

She struggled to keep up with him as they crossed the parking lot. She wasn't used to wearing heels, and only his firm grip on her hand kept her from falling flat on her face. She could see his truck, and her heartbeat cranked up. She was about to have sex with Thomas in his truck, and the thought of being under his large body made her so horny she could barely breathe. She had dreamed about this for years, had wondered what –

She frowned when he dragged her past his truck and kept stomping through the parking lot. Where was he going? Was he taking her to the trees that grew across the left side of the parking lot? It was cold, her breath plumed out in front of her, but she decided she didn't care. She'd take Thomas anyway she could get him, and if that meant freezing her ass off while she did, so be it.

"How much have you had to drink?" He glanced at her.

"Only one beer. Why?" She frowned as he stopped in front of her old but reliable truck.

"Because there's no way in hell I'm letting you drive home drunk," he said.

"Thomas, I thought we were going to…"

"What happened in there was a mistake, Evelyn. A temporary moment of insanity on my part."

She dropped his hand as hurt washed over her. "Whatever, Thomas. Goodnight."

She started back toward the bar, and he took her arms and spun her around gently. "Where do you think you're going?"

"Back to the bar." She arched her eyebrow at him. "Do you have a problem with that?"

"You're damn straight I have a problem with that," he said. "Those guys in there are looking for nothing more than…"

"Nothing more than what?" She asked when he trailed off. "You're one of those guys, apparently, so why don't you tell me what they're looking for."

"I'm not," he said. "I just go there for an occasional beer."

"Oh, is that right?" She rolled her eyes. "Of course, it's just for a beer. You would never be out for a night of casual sex, would you, Thomas? Not you. Always so perfect and willing to bend and do whatever my dad wants you to do. You wouldn't dream of a night of meaningless sex."

He flushed, and she leaned closer to him. "Are you more bothered by the fact that I came to the bar looking to get laid by a stranger or that I didn't come to your guesthouse begging you to fuck me like I did when I was eighteen?"

His nostrils flared, and she grinned at him. "Sorry, Tommy. You lost your chance."

He flushed at the mention of her father's childhood nickname for him, and her grin widened. "It was the bad boy I wanted, and now you're just way too dependable and boring for me."

She watched his iron-clad control snap with something that felt a little like glee. He pushed her back against the truck, pressing his erection against her and staring down at her.

"You certainly seemed to want this back in the bar," he growled.

"A temporary moment of insanity on my part," she said.

He snorted with anger and backed away. "Where are your keys? You're getting into your truck and driving home, Evelyn. No more games."

She glanced down at her cleavage. "In there."

"What do you mean in there?"

"I mean in there." She pointed to her tits. "Do you see pockets on this outfit, Thomas? My truck key is in there."

* * *

THOMAS DIDN'T KNOW WHAT THE HELL HAD GOTTEN INTO Evelyn, but he was torn between turning her around and spanking her or pushing her back against the truck and kissing her until she was moaning his name. "Get the key and get in the truck, please."

"Nope. I'm going back to the bar."

"Evelyn!"

She cocked her head at him. "Tell you what, Thomas. If you're brave enough to go searching for the key and find it, I'll get in my truck and drive myself home to my apartment."

She stared at him, and when he didn't move, she giggled and started to saunter away. He growled in frustration before reaching out and snagging her around the waist. She stumbled back against him, and he groaned in her ear when her soft ass pressed up against his cock. His erection, which had finally started to go down, immediately turned rock hard again.

"Stop playing games, Evelyn. You don't know what you want." He spoke into her ear, grimly ignoring the way she rubbed her ass against his cock.

"I'm not playing games. And I think one of those boys in

there will be glad to help me figure out what I want. In fact, I'm sure of it."

Anger flared in him at the thought of one of those men touching her, undressing her, *fucking* her. He accidentally squeezed her so tightly that she gasped.

"I will go looking for that key myself. I swear to God," he warned her as he relaxed his grip.

His warning had no effect. Evelyn pressed her ass more firmly against his cock and reached behind her. She wrapped her arms around his waist so that her back arched and her breasts pushed out.

"Do what you have to do, Thomas," she purred.

"Please, Evelyn," he suddenly pleaded. "Get the key yourself."

"No."

He blew out his breath. It stirred her hair, and he used one hand to push her hair back over one shoulder and out of his way before looking over her shoulder. The air was cold, and she shivered delicately against him, but he knew the skin covered by her bustier would be warm. Warm and soft and inviting.

He reached down and paused. "Right or left?"

"Take a guess." She leaned against him, her head on his broad chest, and looked at the clear night sky. "But I don't have all night. Either go fishing or don't, big guy."

He slid the fingers of his right hand down the left cup of her bustier. His fingers skimmed across the side of her breast, the skin as warm and soft as he had imagined, and he bit back his groan at her soft gasp of pleasure.

His fingers brushed against something, and he grasped onto the edge of it, pulling it triumphantly from the cup of her bra. He stared blankly at the twenty-dollar bill wrapped around her driver's license.

"Oh look, you've won twenty bucks. Congratulations!"

She grinned up at him before squeezing his waist again. "You want to keep fishing, cowboy? Or can I go back to the bar now?"

He stuffed her driver's license into his pocket and slid his hand into the right cup of the bustier. His hands trembled badly, and his cock was impossibly hard as he searched for long minutes along the side of her breast.

There was nothing, and he wiggled his hand between her breasts, searching the dark, warm crevice for the feel of the key as she lazily rubbed herself against his erection.

"Evelyn?" he croaked out, his throat dry and dusty as the desert. "Are you lying to me?"

When she spoke, her voice was hoarse too. "No. Maybe you should check under them. Things have a way of... migrating in there."

He reached for her right breast, and she cleared her throat. "Better check both sides, Thomas. I can't seem to remember which side I put the key in."

He closed his eyes, muttered something that sounded half like a curse and half like a prayer, and stuck both hands into the cups of her bustier. The lingerie was extremely tight, and, still keeping his eyes shut like a man praying, he wiggled and twisted his fingers under her ample breasts.

He felt a moment of triumph when the tip of one questing finger brushed against warm metal, and he opened his eyes as he pinched the metal between his fingers. All the air whooshed out of his lungs in a single breath.

It had been a mistake to open his eyes. The bustier was tight, with her breasts barely tucked into it, to begin with. The added pressure of his fingers had pushed the firm flesh of her breasts upward until her nipples popped free.

Pink, he thought dimly. *Her nipples are pink.*

He wouldn't admit to himself that he had, on more than one occasion, wondered what colour her nipples were. They had tightened in the cool air, and like a man moving underwater, he dropped the key, cupped her breasts, and lifted until both pale globes were completely free of the bustier.

She didn't object, and he gently grasped her nipples with his forefingers and thumbs. He tugged lightly, and she arched her back and sighed his name. He pulled again before rolling them between his fingers, marveling at how they hardened under his touch. She cupped the back of his neck, tugging his face toward her upturned one.

"Kiss me, Thomas," she begged.

He dipped his head and swept his mouth across hers in a brief, gentle touch. She moaned and parted her lips. "Again."

He cupped her breasts, her nipples hard pearls against his palms, and kissed her again. This time, he slipped his tongue deep into her mouth. She tasted like honey and sin and everything he'd always wanted.

She dipped her hand into her bustier and pulled the key out as he continued to kiss her. He sucked on her lower lip, his callused hands rubbing and massaging her breasts, and she moaned and pulled away. She unlocked the driver's door and wrenched it open.

"Here, Thomas," she whispered. "Take me right here."

He shuddered all over and lifted her into the truck until she sat on the seat with her legs dangling down. The steering wheel dug into her hip, and she whacked her skull on the top of the door frame as she leaned out to kiss him, but she didn't seem to notice.

She wrapped her legs around his waist, dragging him closer to her. She pulled off his cowboy hat, dropped it on the seat behind her, and ran her fingers through his short, dark hair. He kissed her neck, his tongue tasting her soft skin before he nipped lightly on her earlobe.

"Evie," he whispered into her ear. She made a low moan, her body trembling against his. He never called her by her nickname. It had always felt too intimate, too personal. Especially since he tried like hell to keep things almost painfully formal between them.

"Thomas, please," she moaned as he put one big hand on her thigh and slid it under her skirt.

Light splashed across them, and he instinctively pulled her against his chest, hiding her naked breasts. They squinted and put up their hands to block the light from the oncoming car. The car was packed full of men and women barely out of their teens. They honked and hollered good-naturedly out their open windows. "Get a room, you two!"

As the car pulled out of the parking lot, Thomas pulled free of Evie's arms and legs. Like a man waking from a dream, he shook himself and stared horrified at her.

"Evelyn, I'm sorry. I can't – I shouldn't have done that."

"Don't, Thomas. Don't say you shouldn't have." She frowned at him. "Come back to my apartment tonight."

He shook his head, his gaze dropping to her naked breasts before skittering away again. "No, Evelyn. This should never have happened. Your father would kill me if he knew."

She pushed her breasts back into the bustier angrily. "Who cares what my father thinks?"

"I do," he said.

She swung her legs into the truck - he caught a heart-stopping glimpse of her panties as she did - and stuck the key into the ignition. She threw his cowboy hat at him, and he caught it easily.

"Evelyn -"

"Goddamn you, Thomas Sinclair!" she shouted and slammed her door shut before driving out of the parking lot.

He jogged quickly to his truck and climbed in. He followed her home, stopping his vehicle on the street and letting it idle as he watched her park and climb out of her truck. She didn't look at him. She just hurried around to the side of the house and climbed the narrow, metal staircase that led to her apartment door. She took the key from under the flowerpot on the small landing and let herself into her apartment. The lights flooded on, and she stalked across the room and drew the curtains closed.

He sighed and drove back toward the ranch. Christ, he had really fucked up this time.

CHAPTER 3

Thomas cocked his head. He could hear a vehicle approaching the ranch, and he left the barn, walking toward the two men who climbed out of the truck. He shook both of their hands.

"Hello, Paul. Hello, Aaron. It's good to see you."

"Thanks, Mr. Sinclair. And thanks for getting us this job," Aaron said.

"Don't thank me. It was Mr. Crawford who had the final say." He motioned for them to follow him toward the back of the house. The house initially had a large sunroom off the back, but it had been converted to an office nearly seven years ago.

His pulse sped up, and he took a deep breath. Evelyn would be in there, and he had no idea what she would say or do when she saw him. She hadn't been to the ranch on Saturday or Sunday. It was unusual but not entirely unheard of behaviour for her, and her father hadn't seemed concerned about it.

He led the two men up the steps to the office and into the bright, cheery space. The reception area was separated from the office by a chest-high counter that ran the room's length. A swinging half-door at the counter's far end provided access to the office area.

Evelyn was nowhere to be seen, and he was just about to call her name when he heard a soft string of curses. He, Paul, and Aaron peered over the counter. Evelyn was bent over her desk with her ass in the air, reaching between her desk and the wall.

She cursed again and wiggled further onto her desk. Thomas stared at her ass in her tight jeans, and his cock hardened against his worn jeans. Evelyn gave a soft triumphant shout and slid back across the desk, stapler in hand.

Thomas glanced at the men beside him. Paul watched Evelyn with a bored look, but Aaron stared delightedly at Evelyn's full ass. Thomas cleared his throat loudly. Evelyn shrieked, bounding up from the desk and slamming the top of her head against the desk lamp. The lamp rocked on the desk and then fell. The light bulb exploded with a loud bang, and Evelyn rubbed her head as she whipped around and glared at the three men. "What the hell?"

Aaron slipped past the swinging door and stood in front of Evelyn. "Whoa. Are you okay, beautiful?"

"Yeah," Evelyn said, her face pink with exertion and embarrassment.

"Let me see." Aaron scrutinized the top of her head, threading his fingers through her blonde hair.

"No blood. I think you'll live." He grinned at her, and jealousy coated Thomas like thick mud when Evelyn blushed.

"Thanks for checking."

"I'm Aaron." He held out his hand, and she shook it briefly.

"I'm Evelyn. Nice to meet you, Aaron."

With jealousy still pulsing through him, Thomas pushed

past the gate and stood beside Evelyn. "Do you need to go to the hospital?"

She frowned at him. "Hardly, Thomas."

He pulled her driver's license, still wrapped in the twenty, from the back pocket of his jeans. He handed it to her without speaking, although a big – and incredibly immature – part of him hoped Aaron took it as a sign that Evelyn was unavailable.

She snatched it from him quickly, her face turning pink again as she glanced at Aaron. She shoved it into her jeans pocket and stepped back, putting some space between her and Thomas, before smiling at Aaron. "You must be one of the new hires."

"Yes, ma'am." Aaron took off his cowboy hat and grinned at her.

"Call me Evelyn." She dusted off the front of her shirt and smoothed her hair as Aaron and Thomas stepped past the swinging door and into the reception area.

She reached across the counter and shook Paul's hand before taking some papers from the top drawer of the file cabinet. She helped Paul and Aaron fill them out as Thomas studied her closely.

He didn't think it was his imagination that her jeans were tighter than usual, and the buttons on her blouse were unbuttoned further than usual. Her dark blue shirt strained at her breasts and hugged the curve of her stomach. Another almost unbearable surge of jealousy hit Thomas when she stretched over the counter to help Paul, and Aaron stared at her exposed cleavage.

He had to fight the sudden urge to drag Aaron out of the office. Shit, he was losing his mind. Evelyn didn't belong to him. Years ago, when Evelyn was sixteen, her father asked him to watch out for her and help him keep the ranch hands that were constantly coming and going away from her.

"They're not the type of men I want for my little girl," Carl had said. "Can I trust you'll watch out for her when I'm not around?"

Carl, who had treated him better than his own father ever had, meant the world to Thomas, and he had promised to watch out for Evelyn. He knew that at twenty-eight, Evelyn could make her own choices regarding men, but old habits died hard.

And that's all his reaction to Aaron's obvious interest in Evelyn was, he told himself. It had nothing to do at all with his own want for her. In fact, he decided that Friday night in the bar's parking lot really *had* just been a temporary moment of insanity for him. He knew that Evelyn wanted him. She'd made it clear that night in the guesthouse all those years ago, but his respect for her father kept Thomas from revealing his own need for her.

Of course, he'd thought her crush on him had dissipated over the years. She'd returned from college and been friendly but distant with him. Her coolness toward him, after years of adoration, had bothered him more than he would admit. But until two nights ago, she'd never made any type of advance toward him. The sudden return of her interest, seeing her half-naked and kissing her amazingly soft mouth, had taken him by surprise, that was all.

"Thomas?" Evelyn's soft voice dragged him back to the present.

"Yeah?"

"I asked if you would show Paul and Aaron their beds in the bunkhouse, or do you want me to?"

"I'll do it," he said. He didn't want Evelyn anywhere near Aaron's bed.

* * *

"Hello, Evie."

Evelyn looked up from the laptop. "Hey, Dad."

"How was your weekend?"

"It was fine," she mumbled, blushing a little.

He stared at her for a moment before sitting in the rickety wooden chair across from her desk. "Get up to anything special?"

For one black moment, an image of Thomas' fingers pulling at her nipples flashed through her head. She cleared her throat roughly. "No, not really. How about you?"

"No. Michelle and I went for dinner Saturday night at the new restaurant in town."

Michelle was her father's new wife. Evelyn got along well with her. Not that surprising, considering Michelle was only five years older than her.

"That's nice." She stared at her computer screen.

"What are you up to?"

"Trying to book my hotel for that payroll seminar I'm going to in Hinton this week." She smiled at him before gathering her hair into a ponytail and securing it with the elastic band around her wrist.

"Right, I forgot about that." Her dad picked at his nails for a moment. "I'm thinking of sending one of the ranch hands with you. It's a long drive, and I don't like the idea of you driving that far alone."

She sighed. "I'll be fine, Dad. It's not that far of a drive."

He shrugged. "Still, I'd feel better if someone went with you. Besides, there are some horses that I want him to look at while he's there. Can you book another hotel room?"

"Fine. Who are you sending?" She peered at her father. He stared at her with an odd look, and she wondered if Thomas had said something to him about Friday night.

He couldn't have, she thought. He didn't want her father to know something had almost happened between them.

"What?" she asked.

"Nothing." He straightened some papers on her desk. "I think I'll send that new guy Aaron with you."

"Really?" She arched her eyebrow at him, a little surprised that he was willing to send a stranger on a road trip with her.

"Yeah. He comes highly recommended from Lawrence Miller – you remember him and his wife Becky, don't you?"

At her nod, he continued. "Anyway, Larry says he had a good head on his shoulders and an excellent eye for horses. I figure this'll be a good test for him."

"Sure, that's fine with me." She changed her booking, hit the enter button, and waited patiently for the reservation to be accepted.

"Good, good." Her father seemed to want to say something else, and she stared at him expectantly, but he just rubbed at his chest and stood up. "I'll talk to Aaron and let him know."

* * *

"Carl, do you think that's a good idea?" Thomas frowned at the older man.

"What do you mean?"

"We don't know anything about this guy, and you're sending him on a road trip with Evelyn." Thomas lifted a bale of hay and tossed it into the back of the pickup truck. "He's only been working for you for three days. Maybe I should go with her instead."

Carl stared at him shrewdly. "Larry Miller had nothing but good things to say about Aaron. And I'm curious to see if he has as good of an eye for horses as Larry says he does."

The old man took off his cowboy hat and inspected it carefully. "Evie will be just fine with him. Larry says he's trustworthy."

Thomas just grunted in reply, pulling off his gloves and sticking them in the back pocket of his jeans. His gut burned with something he recognized reluctantly as jealousy, but there was no way he could protest further. Carl might be getting up there in age, but he was as sharp as ever. It would rouse Carl's suspicion if Thomas continued to object to sending Aaron with Evelyn.

"I've already spoken to Aaron about it, and he's happy to go," Carl said.

"I bet he is," Thomas muttered.

"What was that?" Carl frowned at him.

"Nothing. When are they leaving?"

"Early tomorrow morning. Evie says the payroll seminar starts at noon on Friday, and if they leave by seven, she'll get there about an hour or so before it starts. Aaron can look at the horses while she's in the seminar, and they can head back Saturday morning."

"Saturday morning?" Thomas jerked in surprise. "They're staying overnight?"

"Yeah. The payroll seminar doesn't end until after six, and Evie would rather stay the night than drive back," Carl said.

Mark rounded the corner of the large barn that housed most of the horses on the ranch. "Hey, boss? I think Star is favouring his front leg a bit. Do you want to look at it, or should I call Doc Hudson?"

Carl shook his head. "Nah, let me take a look at it first." He followed Mark into the barn.

Thomas grabbed another hay bale, wincing when the rough strands bit into his bare hands. With a loud grunt, he tossed it into the back of the truck next to the first bale. He tried hard not to think about Aaron and Evelyn driving to Hinton together and going for dinner after the payroll seminar. Aaron would order drinks for them, maybe even get Evelyn tipsy, and then walk her to her hotel room. His hands squeezed into fists as he pictured Aaron inviting himself into her room, kissing her, and -

"Hey, Thomas."

He turned to see Aaron coming out of the barn.

"Aaron," he grunted.

"Did you hear I'm taking a road trip tomorrow with Evie?" His casual use of her nickname set Thomas's teeth on edge.

"Yeah, I heard."

"I'm looking forward to it. Evie's a pretty girl, and I'd like to get to know her better." Aaron shoved the second hay bale to the back as Thomas threw a third into the truck bed.

He removed his hat, wiping the sweat from his forehead before eyeing the younger man. "Can I give you a word of advice, Aaron?"

"Sure."

"Stay away from Evelyn. Carl doesn't care much for having his ranch hands sniff around his daughter."

"Is it Carl that doesn't care for it or you, Thomas?" Aaron asked.

"I watch out for Evelyn because she's like a sister to me," Thomas said with a surly look at him.

Aaron laughed. "I've seen the way you look at her. There's no way you think of her as a sister."

Thomas glanced at the door to the barn. "You're new, so I'll cut you some slack, but believe me when I tell you that going after Evelyn is a very bad idea. Stay away from her. Do you hear me?"

Aaron dusted off his hands on his jeans and started for the bunkhouse. "Evie's a grown woman. I'll let her decide if she wants me to stay away from her."

He strode off whistling as Thomas glared at him, a mixture of anger and jealousy coursing through his veins.

* * *

"So, Miss Evelyn. What do you like to do for fun?"

Evelyn glanced away from the road and smiled at Aaron. "I don't have a lot of time for fun. It's busy at the ranch."

"That's a shame," Aaron drawled. "A pretty girl like you should have fun occasionally."

Evelyn grinned. They had been driving for over three hours, and she enjoyed Aaron's company. He was charming and funny and amused her with stories about working at the Miller's ranch.

Over the last hour or so, his questioning had become more personal. He was obviously interested in her, and she debated whether she was interested in him. He was handsome enough. He was tall and lean with shaggy blond hair and dark brown eyes. He had a gorgeous smile, and his ass certainly filled out a pair of jeans nicely.

She frowned slightly. Last week at this time, she would have been all over him. But that had been before she had nearly fucked Thomas Sinclair in the parking lot of some seedy bar. Her face flushed. Goddammit, would she ever get the memory of Thomas asking her what kind of panties she was wearing out of her head?

She took the exit into Hinton and smiled again at Aaron as he cleared his throat. "So, what's up with you and Thomas?"

Her truck weaved on the road. "What do you mean?"

He shrugged. "I mean, are you two an item?"

"No, of course not. He's my stepbrother."

"Really?" Aaron stared at her in surprise.

"Well, ex-stepbrother," she admitted. "His mom and my dad were married briefly about twenty years ago."

"I see." Aaron looked out the window. "And the guy just decided to stick around?"

33

Evelyn shrugged. "He left with his mom when she and my dad divorced but returned a year later. He liked the ranch work, and my dad was happy to have him back."

"Interesting," Aaron said.

"Why are you so -" The shrill ring of her cell phone between them made them jump.

Aaron glanced at it. "Speak of the devil. Want me to answer it?"

"Yes, please."

Aaron picked up her cell phone and hit the answer button. "Hey, Thomas." He listened for a moment. "She's right here. I answered her phone because she's driving."

He covered the mouthpiece and grinned at her. "He's worried I've done something untoward with you."

She laughed as he turned back to the phone. "What was that? No, no, she's perfectly fine. We just believe in safety first, you know. No distracted driving in this truck."

She grinned again as Aaron winked at her. "Can I pass a message on to her for you?"

He listened for a moment, said goodbye, and ended the call. "Mr. Sinclair would like you to call him when we get to Hinton."

"Did he say why?"

"He did not. He did, however, seem upset that I was answering your cell phone." He gave her another boyish grin.

She snorted in reply. She had no intention of calling Thomas Sinclair. It would be work-related, and it could wait until Monday.

CHAPTER 4

Thomas rechecked the time. It was nearly midnight on Friday night, and he hadn't heard a word from Evelyn. He paced the small bedroom of the guesthouse for what felt like the hundredth time.

His imagination had been going wild for the last two hours, picturing Aaron and Evelyn having dinner together before returning to the hotel. He could easily imagine Evelyn inviting him into her hotel room. He could practically see Aaron pulling off the tight pink t-shirt she had been wearing when they drove away this morning and peeling down her jeans until she stood nearly naked in front of him.

He dropped down on the bed and covered his eyes with his arm. What he was thinking was ridiculous. Evelyn wasn't the type of girl to hop into bed with some guy she barely knew.

Are you sure about that? Last Friday night, you found her at the bar, ready to take home a random man for a night of meaningless sex. What stops her from deciding Aaron is the guy she wants to invite into her bed?

He reached for his cell phone. He couldn't take it anymore.

* * *

The ringing of her cell phone dragged Evelyn from sleep. She reached clumsily for it and hit the answer button without opening her eyes.

"Hello?"

"Evelyn, it's me."

"Me who?" Her brain wouldn't focus.

"It's Thomas."

"Thomas?" She squinted at the alarm clock. "It's nearly midnight. Why are you calling me?"

"You were supposed to call me hours ago," he said.

"I forgot."

"You forgot?" He took a deep breath. "I've spent the last twelve hours thinking that you were -"

"Were what?" She flopped back on the bed and tried to force the sleep from her brain. "I was in a payroll seminar all afternoon."

"And this evening?" he snapped.

"This evening, I had dinner with Aaron." She rubbed at her eyes. "What is going on with you?"

"Is he in the bed with you right now?" he said.

She pulled the phone away and stared at it for a moment. Faintly, she could hear Thomas talking, and she put the phone back to her ear. "What was that?"

"I asked if that asshole Aaron was in your bed," he barked.

"Are you jealous?" She curled up under the covers. She was wide awake now.

"No," he bit out.

"Then why so interested in who may or may not be in my bed at this very moment?"

"Just tell me if he's in bed with you, Evelyn," he demanded.

"And if he is in my bed?" she asked. "What are you going to do about it, Thomas?"

"I'll drive to Hinton and beat the shit out of him," he snarled.

* * *

Evelyn's low and husky laugh came through the phone, and Thomas's cock hardened at the sound.

"Well then, I guess it's lucky for Aaron that I'm all alone in this big bed," she said.

He released his breath in a harsh rush. Relief poured through him, dousing out the flames of jealousy that threatened to consume him.

"The hotel is nice." Her voice was like a caress against his skin. "I have a lovely king-sized bed. I'm not used to having so much room to spread out. I'm used to my tiny double bed. There would be plenty of room for another person in this bed."

She sighed, and he could hear the rustle of the sheets as she shifted. "Of course, there is something to be said about sharing a small bed. It's been my experience that all that forced skin-against-skin contact while you're sleeping often leads to other bedtime activities."

He closed his eyes. It was too easy to imagine being pressed against Evelyn in her bed. Way too easy to see his hand reaching around to cup her breast and stroke her pink nipple.

He opened his mouth to tell her goodnight and instead said, "What are you wearing, Evelyn?"

He could hear the smile in her voice. "A tank-top and panties. It's cold in the room. I probably should have worn a warmer shirt."

He closed his eyes. The image of Evie lying in bed with her nipples hard and straining at the thin fabric of her shirt sent a spike of pleasure straight to his dick. He could see himself hovering over her, his mouth sucking on her nipple through her tank-top until the fabric was wet and sticking to her.

"Thomas?"

"Yeah." His cock chafed against his jeans, and he pulled at the front of them, trying to relieve some of the pressure.

"I thought maybe you had hung up."

"No. Describe your panties." His voice was rough with need.

"They're just a pair of white cotton panties. They have yellow flowers on them." He heard the rustle of fabric again, and he rubbed at his cock through his jeans.

"Are you taking them off?" he rasped.

"No, just checking that the flowers are yellow. They are," she said cheekily. "What are you wearing, Thomas?"

"My jeans."

"Anything else?"

"No."

"Mmm." She made a small moaning sound, and he rubbed at his cock again.

"Are they the jeans with the rip in the knee?" she asked.

"Yeah. Why?"

"They're my favourite. Unzip them," she said.

"Evelyn…"

"Do it, Thomas. Right now."

He flicked open the button and unzipped his jeans until his cock sprang free.

"Touch yourself, Thomas."

"Evelyn, this isn't -"

"Do you know what I'm doing right now?" she asked.

"What?" he groaned.

I'm pulling on my nipple and pretending it's your hand that's touching me." She made a soft gasping sound that went straight to his dick.

He groaned again and wrapped his hand around his cock, rubbing back and forth.

"Are you touching yourself, Thomas?"

"Yes," he moaned.

"Does it feel good?"

"God, yes."

"Good. Close your eyes. I want you to picture me sliding my hand down my body. I'm spreading my thighs and slipping my hand into my panties."

Her voice was sweetly hypnotic, and he stroked harder and faster. Christ, he was so close already.

"Now I'm touching myself, running just the tips of my fingers over my clit. It feels so good, Thomas." She made another soft moan. "I'm so wet."

"Evie…" Her name escaped his lips in a low guttural groan, and then he was coming all over his hand and his jeans. He panted harshly into the phone. "Fuck, Evie, that felt so fucking good."

"Good night, Thomas." She ended the call before he could respond. He stared blankly at the phone in his hand. What the hell just happened?

* * *

"Mark?" Thomas frowned at the two empty stalls. It was Sunday evening, and he had been doing one last check of the barn when he came across the empty stalls.

"Yeah, boss?" Mark's voice was muffled behind the large walnut-coloured horse he brushed.

"Where are Oakley and Autumn?" He pointed at the two stalls.

"Aaron and Evie took them for a ride." Mark rubbed the horse's muzzle when it turned and nuzzled at his shirt pocket.

"What? When?" Thomas grimaced.

Mark shrugged. "I dunno. A while ago. Aaron said they were going on a picnic."

"How long was a while ago, Mark?" Even he could hear the anger in his voice.

Mark hesitated. "Like, maybe three or four hours?"

Thomas gripped the wooden boards of the stalls so tightly that they creaked. He'd spent most of Saturday afternoon debating whether or not to sneak over to Evelyn's apartment. Just reliving their phone sex in his head, the way she had moaned when she touched herself had gotten him so hot he'd been walking around with half a hard-on since Saturday morning.

She and Aaron had returned around noon on Saturday. She hadn't stayed at the ranch. He'd specifically watched for their arrival so he could be outside when she drove in, but she hadn't even gotten out of her truck. She just dropped off Aaron and drove away without looking at him.

He called her late Saturday evening, but her phone was turned off, and he didn't bother leaving a message. What would he say? Hey, I really enjoyed our phone sex last night. Want to try the real thing tonight?

He'd resisted the urge to drive over to her place, reminding himself that not only was he a decade older than her, but he'd promised her father he would watch out for her. Keep her away from men like him. She may no longer be dancing around the ranch with her blonde hair in pigtails and smudges of dirt on her face like she'd done when she was younger, but that didn't mean he could forget his promise to her father.

An image of the very grown-up Evelyn, her hair in pigtails and on her knees in front of him, had flashed across his mind, and he'd slammed his hand on the kitchen counter. He was going to hell. Evelyn was off-limits, always had been, and always would be.

It didn't matter anyway – Evelyn was alone with Aaron right now. They were probably having sex in some field at this very moment. He would get the kid fired, he decided. If there was even a whiff of his scent on Evelyn when they returned, if she even looked the tiniest bit disheveled, he would personally go to Carl and have Aaron kicked off the ranch.

Thomas squeezed the side of the stall again. The muscles in his arms bulged, and he could feel a vein pulsing in the middle of the forehead.

"Thomas – you okay, man?" Mark asked.

"Just fine," he grunted.

His head snapped up. Faintly, they could hear the approaching hoof beats, and Thomas stormed out of the barn, Mark following directly behind him.

* * *

"Uh oh. Your stepbrother looks angry." Aaron grinned at Evelyn as they rode through the gate and approached the barn.

She leaned over to pat Autumn's neck. Thomas stood outside the barn, and even from here, she could see how red his face was.

"What did you do to piss him off, Evie?" Aaron asked with a cheeky grin.

"Me? I didn't do anything." She wrinkled her nose at him. "I'm pretty sure it was you."

"What? I am a model employee," Aaron said. "Why, I did all my chores and even swept the barn before I took the boss's daughter out for a picnic and sunset ride. Plus, I behaved like the perfect gentleman the entire time. What employer wouldn't love me?"

She laughed and rolled her eyes. Aaron was a lot of fun, and she had enjoyed her date with him today, but she knew she'd have to talk to him about being just friends. Despite his charm and good looks, she'd realized halfway through their date this afternoon that she wasn't interested in him.

She sighed and nudged Autumn closer to the barn. It pissed her off. She was well aware that she wasn't interested in Aaron because of Thomas's sudden interest in her. Except, she thought angrily, she had no idea what was going on in Thomas's brain.

After twenty years of treating her like a little kid, he was suddenly all over her. Had he always felt that way and just hidden it well, or had it only taken a short skirt, lingerie, and dirty talk to pique his interest?

She sighed again. He should have been all over her that night in the guesthouse if that was all it required. She'd been wearing a hell of a lot less that night, and he still rejected her.

She'd purposely ignored his phone call on Saturday. The phone sex had been fun, but she wanted the real thing. A big part of her hoped he would show up at her apartment Saturday night. When he didn't, she swallowed her disappointment and accepted Aaron's invitation for a picnic when he called Sunday morning.

She'd spent enough of her life pining after Thomas Sinclair. Making out with her and participating in a bit of phone sex didn't mean that he wanted a relationship with her. He hadn't had a girlfriend in years. He was probably just horny and decided to have a go at the closest sure thing – her.

All of that made perfect sense to her, except here she was – about to tell a handsome, funny guy who genuinely liked her that she just wanted to be friends while the man of her dreams stared at her like he wanted to kill her.

She pulled gently on the reins. Autumn stopped in front of the barn, and Evelyn stroked the horse's neck. Autumn turned and nuzzled her hand affectionately, and Evelyn reached into the breast pocket of her shirt and pulled out half a carrot. She placed it in her hand, and Autumn delicately picked it up before chewing it.

"Hey, Thomas," Aaron said.

He swung out of the saddle as Thomas stomped across the short distance from the barn door to where Evelyn still sat on Autumn's back.

"Good evening, Thomas. How are -"

Her polite greeting was cut off when he reached up and pulled her from the saddle. Autumn snorted nervously and skittered to the side as Evelyn's foot got caught in the stirrup, and she fell against Thomas. He held her weight easily and hauled her free of the saddle and stirrup, setting her roughly on her feet before him. Before she could say anything, he leaned down and inhaled deeply. She gave him a look that suggested he'd lost his mind.

"Did you just sniff me?"

The redness in his face deepened. "No."

"You did. You totally just sniffed me." She paused and looked him over. "Are you drunk?"

"No, I'm not drunk." His blush had deepened to a rich dark red, and he stepped away from her. "And I didn't sniff you."

"Okay, Thomas. Whatever you say." She twirled her finger beside her head and crossed her eyes at him before turning away and leading Autumn into the barn. Aaron, whistling softly, followed her with Oakley.

CHAPTER 5

"Carl, are you listening to me?" Thomas said.

Carl looked up from the forms he studied. They were in Carl's private office in the main part of the house. Usually, he would be in the converted sunroom with Evie, squashed into a small desk only a few feet from hers, but in the last couple of months, he'd spent more and more of his time in his private office.

Thomas could understand why. It was spacious and quiet, with a couch and a flat-screen TV mounted on the far wall. In fact, he'd long suspected that Carl had previously spent most of his time in the office he built for Evie because he wanted to keep an eye on her.

"Yes, Thomas. I'm listening." Carl leaned back in his chair. "I don't understand why you're so anxious to get rid of Aaron. He's a good worker, and there have been no complaints from the other ranch hands about him."

Thomas grunted. "He's been here a week. How do we really know he's a good worker yet?"

"How do we know he isn't?" Carl said.

"Carl, I…" Thomas paused, not sure how to proceed.

Carl made an impatient sound and looked at his watch. "It's Monday, I've got one hell of a headache, and I have a meeting in less than ten minutes. Whatever you have to say – just spit it out."

"I don't like how he looks at Evelyn."

Carl blinked in surprise. "What do you mean?"

"I mean that ever since they went on that road trip, he's been all over her."

Carl arched his eyebrow at him. "All over her? Thomas, they just got back from the road trip on Saturday. It's been a day and a half. That hardly gives him the time to be all over her."

"Did you know he took her on a picnic on Sunday? They were gone for nearly five hours, just the two of them."

Carl stared at the forms before him again, rubbing his forehead absentmindedly, and Thomas's temper frayed. "Carl!"

"Yes, Thomas. I know he took her on a picnic on Sunday. Michelle saw them leaving and mentioned it to me."

"And you're okay with that?" Thomas asked.

Carl shrugged and rubbed his forehead again. "Evie's a big girl. She can take care of herself."

Thomas's mouth dropped open. Carl had gone above and beyond to keep Evelyn from the ranch hands for the last twenty years. He had hovered over her and smothered her and outright fired ranch hands for being too friendly with her. It was something that had pissed Evelyn off to no end but oddly comforted Thomas. He couldn't believe the older man was suddenly acting so blasé about her dating one of the ranch hands.

"Carl, are you feeling okay?" he asked.

"I feel perfectly fine," Carl snapped. "Are we done, Thomas? I know you care for Evie, and I'm glad she has you watching out for her, but we have to let her grow up at some point. Aaron seems like a nice enough fellow. I'm sure she'll be fine."

He stood, and if he noticed how Thomas's mouth hung open, he didn't comment. "I need to talk to Michelle before my meeting. I'll talk to you later."

He left the office. Feeling like a large combine had run over him, Thomas followed him.

* * *

THOMAS CAREFULLY OPENED THE OFFICE DOOR, WINCING A little when it squeaked and peered into the office. He breathed a sigh of relief. Evelyn was nowhere to be seen. He stared down at his hand. The splinter he'd gotten from the damn fence was huge, and he had picked futilely at it for a while before giving up. He needed tweezers. Unfortunately, the tweezers were in the first-aid kit, and the first-aid kit was in the office.

A bathroom was at the office's far end, and the door was closed. Evelyn must be in there. He could grab the tweezers, pull out the splinter, and get the hell out of the office before she was done, like the coward he was.

He shoved the swinging half-door open with his thighs and stood behind the counter, reaching under it to grab the first-aid kit. He rummaged through the large white box until he found the tweezers. The splinter was deep in the palm of his right hand, and he grasped the tweezers awkwardly with his left hand and dug at the sliver of wood.

* * *

FROM HER SPOT ON THE FLOOR BEHIND HER DESK, EVELYN watched as Thomas crept around the counter like a thief and quietly rummaged through the first-aid kit. His back was to her, but she suspected that he either had a splinter or had cut himself. The man forever forgot to wear his gloves.

She glanced at the piles of paper around her. She hated filing with a passion, and consequently, she was always behind in it. Unable to face the towering pile of paper on her desk for another minute, she'd begun the tedious task of sorting it this afternoon. As the hours wore on, she'd run out of sorting space on her desk and the desk her father used and had spread papers out on the floor. She uncrossed her legs and stretched before climbing quietly to her feet. She grinned a little when Thomas cursed softly.

"Need some help?" she said.

He jumped and shrieked like a girl, spinning around to stare at her. His voice was usually so deep that the high-pitched scream brought on a spat of uncontrollable giggling from her.

"What are you doing here?" He glowered at her.

"I work here, remember?" She laughed again.

"I thought you were in the bathroom." He glanced at the closed door.

"Nope." She leaned against her desk and folded her arms under her breasts. Today, she wore a dark green t-shirt with a low neckline and her usual jeans, and it didn't bother her one bit when Thomas's gaze dropped to her cleavage.

"Who's in there?" He thrust his chin at the door.

"No one. Why? Did you come in here looking for a quickie in the bathroom?" She grinned at him. "I'm right in the middle of filing, but I could take a break."

He flushed and turned away. "Hilarious, Evelyn. I have a splinter." He picked at the sliver of wood, grunting in annoyance when his palm began to bleed.

Telling herself she wasn't playing fair, Evelyn walked up behind him and leaned against him, her breasts pillowed against his back and her stomach pressing against his ass. She peered around him at the palm of his hand. "Ouch. Looks painful."

"Yeah," he grunted again.

She watched him shove and tear at his skin with the tweezers. His big body trembled, and she could see sweat forming into little beads at his temple. Still pissed at the way he'd acted on Sunday, she decided it was payback time.

"Here, let me help you." She twisted him around and plucked the tweezers from his hand. She held his hand and leaned over it, peering at the splinter.

"You made it bleed," she said before ripping open a package of gauze. She blotted the blood away and then searched through the first-aid box. She made a small noise of triumph and pulled out a packet of thin needles.

"You have to use the needle to open the skin first before you can grab it with the tweezers," she said.

When Thomas didn't answer, just continued to tremble like he was a scared little kid, she glanced up at him. "What's wrong? Are you afraid of needles?"

* * *

IT WAS ALMOST FUNNY THAT EVELYN THOUGHT HE WAS SCARED of needles when he was, in fact, terrified of his reaction to her. His cock was rock hard, and it took all of his willpower not to push Evelyn against the counter and kiss her senseless. He stared down at her. Her blonde hair was piled on top of her head, and he could smell the faint scent of her shampoo.

"I'm fine," he said. "Just do it."

She started to prick his skin with the pin and then looked up at him with an impish grin. "Before I start this, did you want to smell me again? Because I find it a bit distracting to have you sniffing at my neck, and I figure we should get that out of the way before I dig around in your hand with a sharp object."

The blush rose up his neck before she finished speaking, and she gave her low, throaty laugh.

"I wasn't sniffing you," he said.

"Of course, you weren't, Thomas." She poked at his skin with the pin, using it to tear a small hole in the skin at the end of the splinter. "But let's pretend for a minute that you *did* smell me. Did I smell good?" She smiled at him, stuck the pin in the gauze, and picked up the tweezers.

He swallowed hard. "Yes."

Using the tweezers, she grasped the exposed end of the splinter and pulled it neatly from his flesh. She picked up the antibiotic cream and smeared a thin layer over the minor wound.

"What do I smell like?" She took a Band-aid from the kit and smoothed it over the palm of his hand.

"I – I don't know."

He watched as she raised his hand to her mouth and softly kissed the palm. "There, all better."

A shudder went through his body, and her grin widened. He stepped back and grimaced when his back hit the counter. He was trapped.

"Maybe you should smell me again," she suggested.

She leaned against him, biting her lower lip when his erection pressed against her belly. She slipped one cool hand around the back of his neck. She tugged, and he bent his head until his face was inches from her throat. He took a deep breath, his hands slipping around her to cup her ass and press her lower body firmly against his.

"Well?" Her voice was steady, even with his hands rubbing her ass.

"You smell like violets," he said.

"It must be my body cream. I use it every morning and

every night. I step out of the shower and smooth it all over my wet body. It's better that way – locks in the moisture." She reached for his hand and brought it toward her chest.

"I think it makes my skin soft." She placed his hand on the bare skin of her upper chest. His thumb rested against the pulse that fluttered wildly in her neck. "Do you think my skin is soft, Thomas?"

"Yes," he croaked.

She plucked his hand from her chest and studied it carefully. "Your skin isn't soft."

She traced the palm of his hand, stroking the calluses with the tip of her finger. "You never remember to wear your gloves, do you?"

He shook his head mutely. Until now, he would never have believed that watching a woman stroke his hand would be one of the most erotic moments of his life.

"It's why you have so many scars, and your hands are so rough," she said. "Tell me, Thomas, the women you've slept with – did they complain about your rough hands?"

"Sometimes." He couldn't stop staring at her eyes, at the tiny gold flecks in the left one.

"I wouldn't complain." She licked her bottom lip, letting the tip of her tongue linger there until his eyes dropped to her mouth. "I've always thought the rougher, the better."

He made a noise like a man drowning for air, grabbed her ass, and pulled her flat against his hard body. He bent his head, and she opened her mouth encouragingly, but he stopped with his mouth hovering over hers.

What the fuck was he doing?

* * *

EVELYN WAS CONFIDENT THAT THE ONLY THING KEEPING HER upright was Thomas's hands on her ass. What had started as a fun little game had quickly spiraled into something hot, exciting, and desperately needed. She'd forgotten about her plan to torment and tease and then walk away, and her entire body ached for Thomas's touch.

She could have screamed with frustration when he stopped just short of kissing her. She waited for a second or two and then licked his mouth. He jerked against her, and she licked his mouth again.

"Let me in, Thomas."

He took one deep shuddering breath and then opened his mouth. She slipped her tongue in and had time for one delicate stroke of his mouth before his hard hand cupped the back of her head, and he kissed her hard.

Oh, sweet mother of God. The man can kiss.

Ridiculous - she knew he could kiss. She had tasted him in the parking lot of the bar. But she had a feeling that he'd been holding back that night, and, oh man, she was right.

She didn't like to think much about his past. It had been painful enough to watch him with other women when she was young and in the middle of a heartbreaking crush – she didn't want to relive it.

He'd certainly dated his fair share of women. She did her best to block out any information about his relationships, but about a year after she returned home from college, she drank half a bottle of whiskey and then drunk-dialed Alice. She felt lonely and blue, and she convinced her best friend to tell her everything she knew about Thomas's past relationships.

Admittedly, Alice didn't know much about Thomas' love life.

"I know he never dates anyone for very long," she said. "And Cathy Messen, you remember her from high school, said that Wendy Dallen stalked him for months after he broke up with her, even though they only dated for about a month. Wendy eventually settled for Rich Stutter, but Cathy says Wendy still talks about Thomas like he's some kind of rock star."

"What else?" Evelyn asked. She was quite drunk by then and had somehow ended up sprawled on the floor of the large kitchen of the ranch house, whiskey bottle in one hand and phone in the other.

"Evie, how should I know?" Alice said. "Since you left for college, I've barely spoken to the man."

"But you know the town gossip." Evelyn hiccupped loudly into the phone. "C'mon, Alice in Wonderland – give me the dirt."

"Look, all I know is that he likes the ladies, and the ladies seem to *really* like him. They do what they can to hang on to him, but he never dates anyone for longer than a year. There's a string of broken-hearted women in this town because of him, and, as your best friend, I'm telling you to stay away from him, Evie. I know you still have a crush, but dating him will bring you nothing but heartache, not to mention probably kill your father. You know how your dad feels about you dating ranchers. Besides, Thomas treats you like an annoying kid sister – he always has and always will."

Alice's words had stung Evelyn deeply, and she'd drunk more whiskey until passing out on the kitchen floor. She'd always wondered why women continued to date him if Thomas was known as such a heartbreaker.

Now she knew. It was in the way he kissed. She had never been kissed the way Thomas Sinclair was kissing her now, and she knew instantly why the women flocked to him.

It wasn't his technique. Although the way he alternated hard and deep kisses with soft licks and light sucking on her bottom lip was definitely making her toes curl, it was the way he kissed her as if she belonged to him. The way he kissed her as if there was nothing that mattered more at this moment than tasting her.

She made a soft moan of encouragement and pushed her tongue into his mouth. He sucked on it roughly and then cupped one breast through her t-shirt. He rubbed his thumb along the nipple, groaning with satisfaction at how hard it was.

She ran her hands up and down his back. The large muscles rippled under her touch, and he sighed into her mouth. She wormed her hands under his t-shirt and traced his abs. God, he had an amazing body. It was all taut muscle and warm skin, and she loved the sound of his moan when she slipped the tip of her finger under the waistband of his jeans and he thrust his pelvis against her.

She pulled away from his hot and oh-so-inviting mouth and smiled up at him. "Do you know what I want, Thomas?"

"What?" He stared at her mouth, and she licked her lips for his benefit.

"I want to taste you."

His hand tightened on her breast until it was almost painful. "Evelyn, I…"

The words died in his throat as she dropped to her knees and unbuckled his belt.

* * *

THOMAS STARED AT THE TOP OF EVELYN'S HEAD. HIS LEGS shook, and he glanced out the large bay window in the reception area. No one was walking across the yard or standing near the barn, but he groaned and said, "Evelyn, anyone could come in. This is crazy."

"Totally crazy," she agreed. Her fingers unbuttoned his jeans and then pulled down the zipper.

"I'm serious, Evelyn. Christ – Michelle or your dad could

come in from the house." He looked at the door that connected the office to the rest of the house.

"Yep, they might," she agreed again. She tugged the front of his underwear down, a soft sound of excitement escaping her throat when his cock popped out.

"My goodness." She gave him an admiring look. "You're a big boy then, aren't you?"

"Evelyn…"

Her mouth was so close to his cock. All he had to do was twist his hips slightly, and he'd be in her mouth. He panted harshly and resisted the urge. He had to stop this. He had to –

Evelyn's mouth - her hot and very wet mouth - closed over the head of his cock, and all rational thought was lost.

"Evie!" he moaned as she slid her mouth down his cock. He gripped her head, and with the last shred of his self-control, he started to push her back. She used her tongue to slide along the thick vein pulsing on the underside of his shaft, and suddenly, his hands were pulling her closer.

She sucked hard, bobbing her head back and forth as he panted and moaned above her. She pulled her mouth away, ignoring his low cry of disappointment, and smiled up at him.

"Tell me you've dreamed about this moment, Thomas."

"I have," he admitted immediately. "So many times."

"For how long?"

"Since the night you asked me to take you to my bed." He uttered another little moan when her soft hands stroked him back and forth.

"Good." She leaned forward and licked away the small drop of moisture that appeared at the tip of his cock.

"Is it as good as you imagined?" she asked before licking and sucking on just the head of his cock again.

"Better," he moaned again, his hands tightening in her hair as he tried to urge her forward. "Please, Evie..."

Evelyn opened her mouth wide and took as much of his cock into her mouth as she could. She tightened her lips around him and began a slow, deep rhythm of sucking and licking.

He thrust helplessly in and out of her mouth, and she put her hands on his hips and allowed him to control the pace. She looked up at him, and at the look of pure heat in her eyes, he made another guttural groan of pleasure.

"Evie, I'm going to come," he gasped out. "Stop, honey! Please, I can't hold off much longer."

She didn't reply. Instead, she hummed loudly. The sound made her lips vibrate around his cock, and with a loud shout, he arched his back and came wildly. She kept her lips wrapped around him, swallowing every drop of his come as he shuddered and moaned above her.

She released him and smiled at him as he stared dazedly at her. "Evie, that was.... I mean, that was so damn -"

He caught movement out of the corner of his eye and turned, his eyes widening with horror. "Jesus Christ! Michelle is here!"

Evie popped up from behind the counter and looked out the window. Michelle had just parked in front of the office and was climbing out of the car.

She grinned at Thomas. "Zip up, cowboy. I'm going to freshen up in the bathroom."

Thomas fumbled with his pants as Evie strolled to the bathroom and disappeared inside. He had just buckled his belt when the door opened, and Michelle walked in.

He leaned against the counter and tried to breathe normally.

"Hi, Thomas."

"Hey, Michelle." His voice was raspy, and he cleared his throat as she gave him an odd look.

"Is Evie here?"

He jerked his head toward the bathroom. "She's in there."

"Okay. Thomas, are you feeling okay?" Michelle said.

The door opened, and Evelyn, her cheeks flushed and eyes sparkling, stepped out. "Oh, hey, Michelle. How are you?"

"I'm good. You're looking lovely, Evie." Michelle returned to studying Thomas as Evelyn joined them.

"Thanks," Evelyn said.

There was a moment of awkward silence, and then Michelle cleared her throat. "I'm running into town and wondered if you needed me to pick up anything. Your dad mumbled something about needing more printer paper."

Evelyn nodded. "We do need more paper. If you want some company, I'll go with you. I need to do the banking anyway."

"Sure. I'd love the company. We can stop for coffee afterward and have some girl talk. Unless you'll be joining us, Thomas?"

Thomas shook his head. "No, I just dropped by to, uh…"

Hot panic bubbled up in his chest as his mind drew a complete blank. All he could remember was Evie on her knees before him and how good her mouth had felt. Why *had* he come to the office?

"He had a splinter in his hand," Evelyn said. "Because he never wears his gloves."

He swallowed. "Yeah, I need to, uh, start wearing gloves because I, uh, have some work to do in the barn. Right now. In the barn."

Evelyn grabbed her purse and a few file folders before pushing through the swinging door and joining Michelle on the other side of the counter. "Ready?"

Michelle nodded as Evelyn glanced back at Thomas. "See you later, Thomas."

"Bye, Evelyn. Bye, Michelle."

Evelyn opened the office door and stepped out as Michelle trailed after her. Before closing the door, Michelle stuck her head back into the office and stared silently at Thomas before grinning. "Wipe the lipstick off your mouth before you return to the barn, Thomas."

CHAPTER 6

H e'd been about to end the call when Evelyn finally answered, her voice hoarse with sleep. "Hello, Thomas."

"Evelyn, we need to talk."

"Thomas, I am not a night owl. You have to stop calling me after midnight. Seriously."

"Did Michelle say anything to you?"

"Say anything to me about what?" she said.

He sighed with frustration. "What do you mean about what? About today! She knows, Evelyn."

"Yup, she does," Evelyn said.

"Shit. Why didn't you tell me your lipstick was on my mouth?"

"Because I didn't notice it either. In case you've forgotten, it wasn't your mouth I was looking at," she said.

His mouth wasn't the only thing that had ended up covered in her lipstick. As his cock stiffened in response to the memory, he said, "I haven't forgotten. Stop distracting me. What are we going to do?"

"About what?"

"Evelyn, you're driving me crazy! Michelle is going to tell your father."

"Thomas, relax. One, Michelle will not say anything to dad, and two, even if she did, who cares? I'm not a child."

"How do you know she won't say anything?" he said.

"Because I asked her not to, and she said she wouldn't. Thomas, besides your mom, Michelle has been my favourite of Dad's many girlfriends/wives. She's not a gossip. She promised not to say anything, and so she won't. You need to relax, big guy. You're going to give yourself an ulcer."

"Are you sure?"

"I'm positive."

"What, uh, what did you tell her?"

Evelyn laughed. "I didn't tell her I gave you a blow job in the office if that's what you're worried about. I don't kiss and tell."

He didn't reply, and she yawned. "Is there anything else I can do for you at this ridiculous hour?"

He hesitated and then reached down and stroked himself. "Are you naked, Evelyn?"

She snorted. "Really, Thomas? I'm not having phone sex with you again."

He flushed a little. "I just wanted to…"

"Wanted to what?"

Just hearing her voice heated his blood. "Dammit, Evelyn. I want to make you come. You've made me come twice, and I still haven't -"

"If you want to make me come, then get your ass over here, cowboy. You know where the key is. Use your delicious mouth for something other than talking," she said.

"I can't," he said. "In six hours, I'll be in a vehicle with that jackass, Aaron. We're taking some horses to Millsview, and on the way back, we're stopping in Hinton to buy the horses he picked out. We won't be back until Thursday night."

"Well, isn't that a shame," Evelyn said.

"Touch yourself, Evie," he said. "Please, honey. I want to hear you come for me."

She made a soft little moan, and he smiled with satisfaction. "That's right, honey. Use your fingers to -"

"I've already told you, Thomas. If you want me to come, you'll have to join me in my bed."

He shifted on the bed. "You know I can't, Evelyn. What's happening between us isn't appropriate and -"

"It's not appropriate for you to join me in my bed, but it's fine to listen to me masturbate over the phone?" He could hear the annoyance in her voice.

"I know I'm being an asshole, but -"

"Good night, Thomas. Have a safe trip. I'll see you Friday. Oh, and Thomas? I am naked."

She ended the call, and he resisted the urge to throw his phone across the room.

* * *

HE STARTED TO SHAKE BEFORE HE EVEN CLIMBED THE STAIRS TO her apartment. It had been three days since he'd seen or talked to her, and he was starved for her touch. He was also tired and frustrated, and more than a little horny. He'd spent two sleepless nights tossing and turning in the hotel bed, resisting the urge to call her and replaying that moment in the office repeatedly in his head.

He'd masturbated repeatedly, but it didn't lessen his need for her like he hoped. Instead, his need burned brighter. What good was his own hand when he'd had Evie's hands on him? When he knew what it was like to have her mouth?

On Wednesday night, Aaron convinced him to go to one of the bars in Millsview. There was a woman there who reminded him of Evelyn. Not in looks. She was a little bigger than Evelyn, with short dark hair and piercings and tattoos, but she radiated the same confidence that Evelyn did. Two weeks ago, he would have been all over her, buying her drinks and seducing her with an easy kind of charm, but now she held zero appeal to him. It was Evelyn he wanted.

He was fooling himself if he thought it was just the last two weeks that had made a difference. Evelyn had returned home from college six years ago, and he hadn't had a single girlfriend in that time. Hell, he hadn't had sex in four. And the last time he had sex, it was a one-night stand with a girl he'd met in a bar a lot like the Millsview bar. He hadn't seen it while flirting with her, but when he woke in her bed in the morning, he'd been more than a little disturbed by the woman's resemblance to Evelyn.

After that night, he had stopped even trying to date. He'd lived the life of a goddamn monk for the last four years, and it was all Evelyn's fault. Why did she have to make it so damn clear that she wanted him? He could have continued to ignore his attraction to her if she had continued with her new coolness toward him. But no, she had to be at that bar, wearing that goddamn lingerie. If she had only kept her hands to herself.

Really? As I recall, she wanted nothing to do with you that night. You forced her to dance with you and then pressed your hard-on against her like a horny teenage boy. You made the first move that night, idiot. Don't kid yourself about that.

Okay, yeah, that was true. But she was ten years younger than him, and his mother and her father thought their relationship was a big brother, kid sister thing. It would freak them both out if they discovered the truth.

He'd finished the other half of his beer, resolving to let this thing with Evelyn go, but this morning, he'd seen the blonde leaving Aaron's hotel room. Aaron stood shirtless in the doorway, kissing the blonde goodbye before giving Thomas a sheepish grin.

"Does Evelyn know you're fucking around on her?" Thomas could barely control the urge to rip off the younger man's head.

Aaron had stepped back. "Calm down, man. Evelyn told me last Monday she wanted to be just friends."

Thomas's anger deflated like a balloon at the knowledge that Evelyn wasn't going to date Aaron. By the time he had Aaron had returned to the ranch, he'd made his decision. He would go to Evelyn, and the two of them would get this thing – whatever it was – out of their systems and return to the way it was before.

They wanted each other because it felt dirty and a bit taboo. They would have sex a few times, the excitement would wear off, and things would go back to normal.

It was a good plan, a fine plan, in fact, and he was sure Evelyn would agree to it. It was why he now climbed the stairs to her apartment, his pulse thudding in his ears, with his cock so hard it was almost painful.

The inner door to her apartment was open, and he stood on the small, narrow landing outside and stared through the screen door. He'd only been to her place a few times for "family" dinners with her father and whoever his current wife was. Thomas had memorized how it looked or, more specifically, how her bed looked.

The front door led into the narrow, alley-style kitchen. It was cut off from the rest of the apartment by a long wall, but a large doorway at the end of the kitchen opened up into the rest of the apartment. It was a small bachelor, but it had an open concept to help offset the slanted ceiling. She'd divided the large area beyond the kitchen into a living room/office and bedroom. A door on the far left wall led to the bathroom. The last time he had been here, nearly two years ago, his gaze repeatedly returned to her neatly made bed and the pink, sheer nightgown thrown casually over the foot of it. After that night, he'd made every excuse in the book to avoid going to her apartment.

Now, nostrils flaring with excitement and need, he stared at Evelyn's ass. She stood in the narrow kitchen, bent over and rummaging in the small fridge. He opened the door without knocking.

She looked up at the soft squeak of the door. "Thomas? What are you -"

He nearly ran toward her. Her eyes widened with surprise when he yanked her away from the fridge and pushed her up against the wall hard enough to make the pictures vibrate.

"Thomas, wait -"

He kissed her, pouring all of his frustration and need for her into one scorching hot kiss. He threaded his fingers through her long hair, pulled her head back, and trailed a biting, sucking path down her throat. God, she smelled good.

Dimly, he was aware of her speaking, of her hands pushing at his hard chest. He captured her wrists and pinned them above her head. He ground his pelvis against her, cupped her jaw, and kissed her again. She tasted like raspberries and vanilla ice cream, and he groaned loudly before sucking on her upper lip.

"Evie, kiss me back," he pleaded against her mouth.

"Mama? Why is that man kissing Aunt Evie?"

Thomas froze and stared wide-eyed at Evelyn.

"I have company," she said.

He turned his head and stared at Evie's best friend, Alice, and her youngest daughter standing in the living room.

"Hello, Thomas." Alice grinned as her little girl leaned against her leg and stared suspiciously at him.

"Hey, Alice."

"It's good to see you again."

"You too." He realized with horror that he was still pinning Evelyn to the wall of her apartment, and he stepped back abruptly.

"Mama, who is that?"

Alice wiped the smears of ice cream from her face. "His name is Thomas, honey. Can you say hello?"

"I don't like him," the little girl announced.

"Darla!" Alice frowned at her as Evelyn snorted laughter.

"Don't say that. Thomas is a very nice man," Alice admonished gently.

Darla looked him up and down, her nose wrinkling. "He smells bad, and his shirt is dirty."

Evelyn pinched her lips together and tried not to laugh as Thomas flushed.

Darla was right. He *did* smell bad, and his shirt *was* dirty. After unloading the new horses into the barn, he had gone directly to Evelyn's. He had been so anxious to see her, to tuck her under him and make her his, that he hadn't even thought about stopping at his house and showering first.

"Hush, Darla," Alice said.

"We just had fruit and ice cream. Would you like to join us?" Evelyn asked.

"Uh, no, thank you. I should probably get going. It's late, and I need to shower and change." Thomas backed away from Evelyn and inched toward the kitchen door.

Smiling, she followed him and leaned against the counter before crossing her arms across her chest.

"Good night, Thomas." She let her eyes drift up and down

his body in a slow caress, and he swallowed hard. "It was good to see you again."

She grinned at him, and he groped behind him for the latch on the screen door. It opened, and he stumbled onto the landing, grabbing the railing for balance.

"Good night, Evelyn." Cheeks burning, he hurried down the stairs.

CHAPTER 7

E velyn leaned against the counter and stared out the window of the office. Thomas walked into the barn with his head bent against the wind. She glanced at her watch. He'd been avoiding her all day. It was nearly five, and she was heading home soon. The other ranch hands would be eating dinner. It was the perfect time to speak to him.

She slipped into her jacket and hiked quickly across the yard to the barn. She heaved open the large door and peeked inside. It was quiet and empty, and she shut the door behind her before walking down the wide aisle. The barn was warm and almost steamy from the bodies of the many horses in their stalls.

She could hear the faint sound of Thomas's voice at the far end of the barn, and she moved steadily toward it. She stopped to pat Autumn, smiling a little when the horse nuzzled her hair with its large, flat nose, and then continued toward Thomas. He stood outside of Star's stall. Star was one of the oldest horses on the ranch. As a child, Evelyn had learned to ride on the giant but gentle beast. Most ranches would have sold him off long ago, but her father had a soft spot for him, and Star would live out his life here. She stopped and watched as Star leaned his head over the stall door and nudged Thomas's chest.

Thomas murmured something she couldn't hear and pulled a carrot from his shirt pocket. He handed it to the old horse. The horse munched it contently as Thomas ran his rough hands over Star's smooth, broad neck. As Evelyn moved forward, his fingers combed out the tangles in Star's mane.

Thomas paused and then continued to comb Star's mane with his fingers. "Hello, Evelyn."

"How did you know I was here?" She hadn't made a sound.

"Violets," he said.

She smiled, secretly delighted that he recognized her scent. "How was your trip?"

"It was fine."

She stood next to him and rubbed Star's broad forehead. "Good. You've been avoiding me today."

"No, I haven't," he said

"Yes, you have."

He glanced at her, his gaze lingering on her mouth, before looking away. "I was busy today."

"Oh. What are you doing tonight?" She leaned against Thomas and tangled her fingers into Star's mane, letting them brush against Thomas's face.

"I... nothing. No plans," he said.

"You should come by." She gave him a slow and inviting smile. "I'll be alone tonight."

"It's not a good idea. I've been thinking all day, and I should not have come by your apartment last night. I know there's this – this attraction between us, but I'm ten years older than you."

"So?"

"So, I'm an old man compared to you."

She scoffed. "Thirty-eight is hardly an old man, Thomas."

"It's not just that. Our parents used to be married, for God's sake. I'm your stepbrother."

"You were – twenty years ago," she said. "Don't take this the wrong way, but you sound like a broken record. And just so you know? I never thought of you as my stepbrother."

"Evelyn." He let his breath out in a harsh rush when she traced her fingers over his hand.

She cupped Thomas's face with her other hand and turned him toward her. "I'm tired of trying to convince you, Thomas. I'll be home alone tonight, and I want you to join me in my bed, but I'm done begging."

She ran her thumb over his bottom lip. "Think about it, okay? If you don't come by tonight, I'll respect your decision and not ask you again."

"Evelyn, I…"

"Think about it, Thomas. Good night." She stood on her tiptoes and brushed her lips lightly against his before walking away.

* * *

Like a man in a dream, he reached under the flowerpot and pulled out the small metal key. He opened the door and slipped quietly inside, locking it behind him. The small apartment was dark, and he wondered if she was in bed. It was nearly eleven, and she must have been convinced he wouldn't show.

He pulled off his cowboy boots with a quiet grunt and left his hat on the counter as he moved deeper into her apartment. The bathroom door was open and casting light onto Evelyn's empty bed. He could hear the faint sound of water lapping at the tub.

His half-hard cock turned to a raging, throbbing erection. He walked silently to the bathroom and peeked into the room. He sucked in his breath. Evelyn reclined in the tub with her eyes closed.

He thought she'd fallen asleep in the tub until he heard her soft moan. The bubbles hid her body, but she moaned again and arched her back as he watched. Her pink nipples broke through the bubbles. He reached down and rubbed his aching cock. The water rippled in the tub as she moaned a third time, and her shoulders moved up and down delicately.

The revelation of what she was doing hit him in a hard, sweet rush. She was touching herself because she had finally given up on him. He moved to the tub, unbuttoning his shirt sleeve and rolling it to his elbow.

As he dropped to his knees beside the tub, he spoke in a low and quiet voice, "Do you need help, Evie?"

She shrieked and jerked wildly, her eyes popping open as water and bubbles splashed over the tub, soaking into his jeans.

* * *

EVEN IF HE WAS THE NUMBER ONE STAR IN ALL HER FANTASIES, the last thing Evelyn expected to hear while masturbating was Thomas's perfect voice. Could you blame her for screaming and spilling water everywhere?

"Thomas! You scared the hell out of me!" She gave him a light smack on his chest, leaving a wet handprint.

"What are you doing here?" Feeling self-conscious, she slipped deeper into the tub.

"You invited me, remember?"

"I thought you'd decided not to take me up on the invitation." For the first time in her life, she felt shy and uncertain.

Thomas, the man she had lusted after for most of her life, had just caught her masturbating in the tub.

"I tried. I couldn't stay away," he said. He wiped away some bubbles from her cheek. "Did it feel good when you were touching yourself, Evie?"

"Yes."

"What were you thinking about while you touched yourself?"

"You. Your hands and your mouth," she said.

He smiled. "I like that."

She watched, mesmerized, as he slipped his hand under the water. He traced his fingers from her knee up to her bare thigh. Her eyelids fluttered closed, and she made a soft, sighing moan as he traced tiny circles on the smooth skin of her thigh.

"Open your legs, Evie."

She let her legs fall open, and Thomas stroked her inner thigh before touching the soft curls between her legs. She moaned again, and he moved his fingers lower and pushed apart her lips until he found her clit. It was swollen and slippery, and he circled it before rubbing firmly.

Her hands gripped the side of the tub until her knuckles turned white and her hips thrust upward. He had just slid one finger into her when her orgasm hit her hard and unexpectedly. Thomas groaned when her pussy clamped tightly around his finger, and she arched her body. The water in the tub crested over the rim, splashing more water onto him and the floor. She fell back in the tub, panting harshly, and her cheeks pink.

"Oh my God, Thomas." She stared at him as he slid his hand out from between her legs and squeezed her bare leg.

"Your water's starting to cool." He stood and reached for the towel hanging off the hook on the wall as she stood.

He stared for so long at her wet, naked body that she

blushed and reached for the towel he held. She wrapped it around her body as he lifted her from the tub. He set her down on the bathmat and kissed her until her knees buckled and she leaned against him.

She squeezed his hand gently before leading him out of the bathroom to her bed. She helped him out of his clothes until he was as naked as her. She dropped her towel and lay back on her bed, parting her legs and smiling softly at him.

He took a deep, shuddering breath. "Evie, are you sure about this?"

Her smile widened. "Yes. I've been waiting for this moment since I was eighteen, Thomas. Don't make me wait any longer."

He took another deep breath and took the condom out of the pocket of his jeans before dropping them back on the floor. He rolled it on and knelt between her smooth thighs. She hooked her legs around his hips and drew him closer as he dipped his head and kissed between her breasts. She was still damp from her bath, and he licked away the small water droplets on her chest and collarbone. She guided his head to her nipple, and he sucked it into his mouth. He sucked hard and then blew lightly on it as her hands threaded into his hair and clenched tightly.

"Please, Thomas," she moaned.

"I want you so much, Evie," he groaned against her breast.

Her hand reached between them, and his breath hissed out between his teeth when she gripped his cock and guided it to her warm, wet slit. "I want you too, Thomas."

He kissed her as he entered her, his tongue pushing into her mouth as his cock pushed into her body. She moaned again, her fingers digging into his back.

He stopped and gave her an anxious look. "Have I hurt you?"

Evie kissed him, nibbling at his lips and then licking his mouth. "No. It feels so good, Thomas. So right."

She braced her feet on the bed and lifted her hips to meet each of Thomas's gentle thrusts. He propped himself up on his hands, and she ran her fingers across his broad chest and over his shoulders.

She lifted her head and kissed his neck, smiling a little at the low groan that tore from his throat. He was moving slowly and gently in her, and she cupped his face and stared into his eyes. "Harder, Thomas."

"Oh God, Evie." He moved in her using hard, deep thrusts that rocked her into the bed and started a throbbing pulse of pleasure deep within her pelvis.

She moaned his name and wrapped her legs around his hips, locking them in the small of his back. He plunged in and out of her, her soft body cushioning his hard one as their hips slapped together in a quick rhythm.

"Thomas!" she gasped out and then arched her back, her entire body shaking wildly against his as she climaxed around him.

He cried out when her inner muscles tightened around his cock and buried his face in her neck as he came inside of her. He collapsed against her, and she wrapped her limbs around him and rubbed his back. After a few moments, he rolled off of her and relaxed on his back. She curled up next to him, and he kissed her forehead.

She rested her head on his chest and listened to the rapid beat of his heart as he stroked her back with his hard, warm hand. She knew without a doubt that he would spend the weekend with her, but that Monday morning, he would tell her they couldn't do this again.

She smiled a little. She had two days to change Thomas's mind and loved a challenge.

CHAPTER 8

"E vie?"

"Hmm?" She continued to rub the body cream into her long legs.

It was early Monday morning. He'd spent the weekend with her and discovered that Evelyn wasn't kidding when she said she wasn't a night person. She was asleep by ten each night and awake by five every morning. He watched as she scooted back on the bed and switched legs. Just watching her smooth the cream into her silky skin gave him another damn erection.

Thomas had thought that after an entire weekend of doing nothing but exploring every delectable inch of Evie's body, he would be satiated. He was wrong. He wanted her more now than before he knew what it was like to be inside her soft body, to hear her moan his name and plead for him to make her come.

She was amazing in bed, open and giving, and so sensual. It made his body heat up just thinking about it. He wanted to take her back to bed, bury himself in her softness and her heat, and not think about anything other than bringing her pleasure.

He had come to Evie's house Friday night after promising himself that it would be this weekend and this weekend only. At the time, it had seemed like a good idea. Now, faced with the prospect of never touching her again and, even worse, watching the hurt flood her face when he told her they couldn't do this again, he couldn't believe what he'd done.

He'd been so anxious to be with her, so desperate to finally satisfy his decades-old need for her with a sex-filled weekend, that he hadn't stopped to think about how it would affect her.

You don't have to end it then. Tell Evelyn you want to keep seeing her if she'd be willing to keep it hidden from her father.

His hands clenched on his jean-clad thighs. He was an asshole. One, Evelyn deserved better than sneaking around her father's back with him, and two, she loved him. He could try to deny it, but he knew full well that she loved him. He had known it for years, and yet he still allowed himself to come to her, to use her, when he knew there was no future for them.

Carl was like a father to him. He had taken Thomas in when his own mother didn't want to deal with him, and he had treated him like a son. If he discovered that Thomas had repaid his years of kindness by banging his baby girl, he'd cut off his balls and feed them to him. Even worse would be the betrayal in Carl's eyes.

Evie had finished with her body lotion and sat quietly on the bed, staring at him. His stomach rolled with nausea – he was about to break her heart. "We need to talk, Evie."

She stood gracefully, paused to take something from her nightstand, and crossed the room to where he sat on a kitchen chair.

"So, talk." She hadn't gotten dressed yet and wore the

same pink sheer nightgown that had tormented him years ago. He groaned inwardly when she straddled him. She rubbed her bare pussy against his jean-covered crotch and smiled at him.

His eyes dropped to her breasts. Her nipples were hard against the fabric, and he was struck with the almost undeniable urge to suck gently on them through the material.

She dipped her head and licked his throat and then smiled when his hands circled her waist.

"Evelyn, please. We really need to talk."

"I know. Go ahead - say what you need to say."

She smiled at him, and he ran his thumb over her swollen mouth and the red patch on her chin. "You have stubble burn."

She traced her mouth. "Do I?"

"Yes. Everyone's going to know what you were up to this weekend. Your mouth is swollen as well."

She pressed her mouth gently against his, and he lapped lightly at her lips with his tongue. "I'm sorry."

"Don't be. I find your stubble sexy."

He leaned back a little, trying to ignore the way she rolled her hips against his pelvis.

"Touch me, Thomas," she said.

"Evie, I can't," he nearly moaned.

"Can't or won't?" She cupped her breast and rubbed her thumb over her nipple in slow circles.

His nostrils flared, and he pushed her hand out of the way and put his hand over her breast, squeezing it roughly.

"That feels so good, Thomas." She licked his mouth again before reaching under her to unbuckle his belt.

"Evie, what are you doing?" he groaned.

"Well, considering that you're about to tell me we can never do this again, I figured I'd show you one last time what you'll miss out on." She kissed his cheek and unbuttoned his jeans.

He pushed her back a little, staring at the condom she held in her left hand. "You knew what I wanted to talk about?"

She smiled a little. "Thomas, honey, you should never play poker. You can't hide a thing on that handsome face of yours."

"Then you know we can't keep doing this," he said.

"I know you believe that," she said. "Of course, I hoped a weekend of me banging your brains out would have changed your mind, but," she shrugged and tugged his cock out of his pants, "c'est la vie, right?"

She stroked and squeezed him as he took a deep breath and struggled to focus. "Evie, maybe we could keep it quiet. If we -"

"If we what, Thomas?" She rolled the condom onto his cock with studious concentration before smiling at him. "Keep it from my dad? I'm not going to do that. I'm twenty-eight years old. That's too old to be hiding a lover from my father."

She leaned forward and kissed his neck. Thomas stared up at the ceiling, his mind reeling. This conversation was not going at all like he thought. He assumed Evelyn would be upset, probably cry, and he would have to explain why he was such a goddamn bastard. Instead, she acted like it was no big deal.

"Thomas? What's wrong?" She frowned at him.

"Evelyn, I thought you would -"

He hesitated, and she raised her eyebrows at him. "Thought I would what?"

"I thought you would be more upset that this was just a one-time thing."

She cocked her head at him. "Why would you think that?"

"Well, because..." He was suddenly profoundly uncomfortable, and his erection had all but disappeared.

"Because what?" she prompted.

"Because you love me," he said

She smiled gently at him. "Both of us are too old to confuse lust with love, Thomas. I've wanted you since I was eighteen, but wanting and loving are two different things."

He couldn't hide his wince, and she cupped his face. "I've hurt your feelings."

"No, you haven't." He stared at her perfect chest, and she tugged on his face until he looked at her again.

"I have. I'm sorry," she said.

He didn't reply, and she scooted a little closer to him. "Thomas, I don't know what you want from me. Considering that you just admitted you only wanted a weekend thing, this should make you happy."

He stared over her shoulder. "I don't want to hurt you."

"You haven't," she said. "I'm a big girl, and I knew what this was when I invited you over Friday night."

She rubbed his cock, and it stiffened again under her touch. She kissed him lightly on the mouth, urging his lips apart so she could explore his mouth with her warm tongue.

"You want more than this. I know you do." He cupped the back of her neck as her soft fingers continued to stroke and squeeze.

She shrugged. "I knew I only had this weekend to change your mind. I tried, and it hasn't worked. I told you before I wasn't going to beg, and I meant that."

She lifted her hips and, without warning, plunged his cock deep inside of her. They both moaned in pleasure, and she braced her feet on the floor as she rode him slowly.

"I'm sorry," he groaned.

"Don't be. You don't want me like I want you – it's not the end of the world."

She pushed the straps of her nightdress down off her arms and slid the soft, silky material to her waist, baring her breasts to him.

"Touch me, Thomas," she demanded.

He lowered his mouth to her breast and suckled lightly on one pink nipple. She arched her back and held his mouth to her breast as he nibbled with his teeth and used the tip of his tongue to tease her nipple.

She rode him harder in response. He put his hands around her waist and held her steady as he arched his hips off of the chair, meeting each of her sweet thrusts. He groaned when she squeezed her inner muscles around his throbbing cock and stared at her flushed face.

"I do want you, Evie – so much," he rasped out before he pulled her body against his and buried his face in her neck. He thrust in and out of her, kissing her throat as he stroked her bare back.

Her soft moans and low cries of ecstasy brought him dangerously close to his climax. When she reached between them and rubbed at her clit, he groaned her name and pumped hard, his orgasm rushing through him as she squeezed around him and cried his name.

She collapsed against him, and he rubbed her back, staring blankly at the ceiling. How the fuck was he supposed to walk away from her?

CHAPTER 9

"Evelyn? Hey – Evelyn?"

Evie stared blankly at Michelle. "What?"

"What do you mean what? I've been calling your name for like five minutes," Michelle said irritably.

Evie stood from behind her desk. She stretched and wandered over to where Michelle was leaning on the counter. "Sorry, my mind was somewhere else."

"It's been there all week," Michelle snapped. "What has gotten into you? Does it have something to do with Thomas?"

"Why would you ask that?" Evie asked.

"Because Thomas has been a miserable bear the last two weeks. He's so bad that even your father has noticed. Did something happen between you two? Did you fight?"

"No. Everything's fine with us."

"Well, I don't believe you, but I don't have time for this right now." Michelle rubbed her stomach.

"Are you okay, Michelle?" Evelyn asked. Michelle was pale, and there were dark circles under her eyes. Plus, it wasn't like her to be so irritable.

"Yes, I'm fine," Michelle snapped again. "I'm assuming we'll see you at dinner tonight? Your Aunt Janice will be there."

Evelyn wrinkled her nose. "I think I might be busy."

Her father's older sister Janice meant well, but Evie was tired of listening to her aunt lecture her on how she needed to find a man, settle down, and give Carl grandchildren.

"Oh, for heaven's sake, Evelyn. She hasn't been to dinner with us in ages, and she's not getting any younger. Besides, it would mean a lot to your father if you joined us." Michelle shot a look at her that would have melted a glacier.

Evelyn held up her hands. "Okay, okay. I'll be there. What time?"

"Just come into the house after work. There's no point in you going home and coming back."

Michelle opened the door that led into the house and then hesitated. She rubbed her stomach again as her expression softened. "I'm sorry, Evie. I didn't mean to be so bitchy."

"It's fine," Evelyn said. "Everyone seems to be grumpy lately. Dad yelled at me for five minutes this morning over what he thought was a payroll error. He didn't even apologize when he realized he was wrong."

"Cut your dad some slack, will you, Evie?" Michelle asked. "He's having a rough time lately."

"Why? What's going on?"

"Nothing. Just give him a break, okay? For me?"

"Okay. Michelle – are you sure *you're* okay?" Evelyn asked.

"Yes. I'm just tired. I'll see you in a few hours."

* * *

"Evelyn, when are you going to get married?"

Evelyn glanced at her watch. She'd been here fifteen

minutes. It was a new record for Aunt Janice. "When I find the right guy, I guess."

The old woman frowned at her and thumped her cane on the wooden floor. "Women these days are too picky. You keep looking for the perfect guy. Take it from me – the perfect guy doesn't exist."

That's where you're wrong, Evelyn thought sourly. The perfect guy was right on this ranch. He just didn't want anything to do with her.

"Dinner will be ready in five minutes." Michelle poked her head into the living room. "Can I get you another drink, Aunt Janice?"

Aunt Janice held her glass out. "Yes, please. I'll take another whiskey neat."

Evelyn suppressed a grin. Aunt Janice smoked cigarettes like she was a 1950s starlet and could drink a lumberjack under the table. Her doctor had tried numerous times to get her to quit both the smoking and the drinking, but he was no match for Aunt Janice's iron will.

Michelle took the glass from Aunt Janice. She stopped, a weird look coming over her face before pressing her hand to her stomach.

"Michelle? Are you okay?" Evelyn started to stand, but Michelle waved her off.

"I'm fine, Evie. It's just a bit of the stomach flu."

"Why don't you sit down? I'll help Dad with the dinner."

"No, no. I'm fine."

She left the room, and Evelyn relaxed in her overstuffed armchair.

"That girl be with child," Aunt Janice said.

Evelyn stared at her. "What?"

"She's pregnant."

"No, she isn't," Evelyn said.

Aunt Janice shrugged. "I know a pregnant woman when I

83

see one, and Michelle is pregnant. You're going to be a big sister, Evie."

"Aunt Janice -"

The front door opened, and Thomas stepped into the living room. He removed his boots and hung his cowboy hat on the coat tree before raking his hand through his short hair. "Sorry, I'm late."

Evelyn's heart ramped up to a minor stroke level. She looked down at the floor. Her stomach churned, and stupid warmth had flooded between her legs. Thomas had avoided her for two weeks, and she'd tried to tell herself it was for the best. But God, she missed him.

"Tommy!" Aunt Janice crowed with delight and held out her arms. "Come give your Aunt Janice a hug."

Of course, Aunt Janice loves him. Everyone loves goddamn Thomas. Her grumpy thoughts weren't exactly kind, but dammit, she was horny as hell over here, and Thomas's tight jeans weren't helping her hooch dampness issue.

Thomas crossed the room and gently hugged her aunt. "It's good to see you again, Aunt Janice."

"You too, dear boy." She patted the spot on the couch beside her, and Thomas sat down.

"Hello, Evelyn." He nodded briefly to her, and she smiled stiffly in return.

Stop it, Evie. You knew what this was. Don't take it out on him.

"How are you, Thomas?" she asked

"Can't complain. How about you?"

"The same."

There, she'd done her duty and made small talk. With another painfully formal smile, Evie grabbed her phone from her pocket and scrolled through Facebook, hoping Thomas would take the hint and stop talking to her.

* * *

THOMAS COULD TAKE A HINT WHEN HE WAS GIVEN ONE. Evelyn didn't want to talk with him, and he couldn't blame her. As Aunt Janice chatted about the weather, he nodded in all the right spots while covertly studying Evelyn. She wore jeans and a loose t-shirt, and she looked fantastic. Her blonde hair was pulled into a ponytail, and her full mouth looked soft and shiny. A memory of kissing those lips, of watching them move their way down his chest, flickered through his mind, and he groaned inwardly and looked away.

He took a deep breath, smelling the sweet scent of violets, and forced himself to concentrate on Aunt Janice.

"Tommy, you need to stop by the house more often. I haven't seen you in ages." Aunt Janice patted his knee.

"Sorry, Aunt Janice. I've been pretty busy lately."

"You found yourself a good woman yet, Tommy?" she asked

"No, ma'am."

Aunt Janice frowned. "Why not? You're handsome enough. Stop being so damn picky, and you'll find someone."

"Yes, ma'am," Thomas said. He glanced at Evelyn again. She was picking at a thread on her jeans and biting her lower lip. He wanted to pull her into his lap and suck and bite on her lip for her. He wanted to take her back to his house, strip off her clothes, and bury his head between her soft, smooth thighs until she was crying his name and coming wildly. He –

Christ! He needed to get control. Sporting an erection at the family dinner wouldn't be at all embarrassing.

He tore his gaze from Evelyn and turned back to Aunt Janice. She studied him with her wrinkly brow furrowed in a way that made him nervous.

She looked at Evelyn and then back to Thomas. He stifled a groan when her eyes lit up and a grin crossed her face.

"Hi, Thomas." Michelle appeared in the doorway leading to the kitchen.

"Hi, Michelle. How are you?"

"Good." She smiled at all of them. "Dinner's ready.

* * *

"THOMAS, I THINK WE SHOULD LOOK INTO A NEW BREEDING program with -"

"Carl," Michelle said. "No talking about work at the dinner table."

Carl frowned. "I've never agreed to that rule, Michelle. I don't see why -"

"Carl." Michelle shook her head at him. "Not tonight, honey. Please."

Evelyn frowned a little. She didn't think the tension between Michelle and her father was her imagination, and she wondered if Thomas or Aunt Janice could feel it.

Michelle turned to her with a strained smile. "So, what's new with you, Evie? You've been leaving the ranch so quickly after work that I feel like we haven't seen you in forever."

Evelyn shrugged. "Not much. I'm thinking of taking a trip."

"A trip?" Thomas paused with a forkful of roast beef halfway to his mouth. "A trip where?"

Evelyn took a sip of water. "I was thinking Europe – maybe do some backpacking."

"Ooh, how exciting!" Michelle folded her hands together and leaned forward. "I've always wanted to go to Europe. How long would you be gone?"

"A month or two."

Thomas choked on his drink of water, and Aunt Janice thumped him on the back.

"A month or two?" Thomas stared at Evelyn. "Who are you going with?"

"I'm going by myself," she said.

"Are you crazy? You can't go backpacking across Europe by yourself. It isn't safe," Thomas said.

She scowled at him. "I'll be fine, Thomas."

"It's too dangerous." Thomas angrily stabbed a piece of roast beef. "Tell her, Carl."

Carl nodded. "He's right, Evie. It's too dangerous for a little girl like you to go to Europe alone."

Evie rolled her eyes. "I'm not a little girl, Dad."

"Yes, well, I still don't think it's a good idea, and I don't want you going," Carl said.

Evelyn clenched her hands under the table and smiled at her father. "Luckily for me, I'm twenty-eight years old, and you don't get to tell me what to do anymore."

Carl glared at her. "So what? Just because you're twenty-eight, does that mean I'm not allowed to give my opinion? I'm supposed to like the idea of my little girl traveling across Europe by herself?"

Her father's voice rose, and as he rubbed at his chest, Michelle put her hand on his arm. "Carl, calm down."

He ignored her. "Evie, I get that you -"

"Dad, we're not doing this," Evelyn said. "Aunt Janice, pass me the butter, please."

As Aunt Janice passed the plate of butter, Thomas glared at Evelyn. "You should listen to your father, Evelyn. He only wants what's -"

"Don't, Thomas," Evelyn said. "You have even less say in this than Dad does."

The hurt look on his face made guilt rush over her. She looked down at her plate, refusing to let her guilt at hurting him make her apologize.

"Thomas is only trying to look out for you." Carl continued to rub hard at his chest.

"I don't need Thomas to look out for me," Evie said.

"Well, you need someone to keep an eye on you. I could

pull up a dozen news stories from the internet about young women like you who went missing while on their grand adventure. If you think I'm going to let my little girl become a news story, you've got -"

"Thomas could go with her," Aunt Janice said.

As Evelyn and the other stared at her, she popped a piece of cheese into her mouth. "What? He could. Then Evie could have her big European adventure and we wouldn't have to worry about her being hurt."

She swallowed the cheese and winked at Thomas. "You'd take good care of her, wouldn't you, Tommy?"

"I… yes, ma'am?" Thomas looked like he had no idea what to say.

Carl snorted. "I can't afford to lose Thomas for an entire month. The ranch would fall apart without him. Besides, Evie and Thomas could never spend a month alone together. They'd kill each other."

There was an awkward silence, and then Michelle stood up from the table. "Who's ready for dessert?"

* * *

"Evelyn?"

Evie jumped and whirled around. She had just come out of the bathroom, and Thomas stepped out of the shadows of the hallway into the light.

"Jesus, Thomas! Stop sneaking up on me." She scowled at him before turning to leave.

He took her arm, gently pushing her up against the wall and pinning her there with his body.

"What are you doing, Thomas?" she said.

"Are you serious about going to Europe?" he asked.

"Yes. It would be nice to get away for a while."

"I don't want you going."

She shrugged. "I don't care what you want, Thomas. Besides, why do you care?"

He frowned. "It's too dangerous, Evie."

"I can take care of myself. Stop treating me like a little girl."

"I know you can, but it's not a good idea to be in a strange country alone."

She sighed again with irritation as he stared down at her. Thomas's stomach rolled with an odd combination of fear and lust. The thought of Evelyn leaving and not seeing her for two months was bad enough, but thinking that she might find someone else while she was gone nearly killed him.

He wouldn't admit how appealing the idea of going to Europe with Evie was. They could explore the country together during the day and explore each other at night. There would be no need to hide their relationship or worry about her father or anyone else catching them. They could just be together.

"Please don't go, Evie," he said. He brushed a strand of her hair back from her face. "Please."

"Don't ask me not to go, Thomas. You have no right to ask me that."

He knew he didn't, but he'd asked anyway and pissed her off. Well… mostly pissed her off. It wasn't just anger in her gaze.

"Fuck," Evie whispered. "You're killing me here, Thomas. Walk away before I push you to the ground and take what I want."

He groaned and slammed his mouth down on hers. She opened her mouth immediately, and their tongues twisted together in a hot, sweet tangle. He shoved his hands under her t-shirt, rubbing and squeezing her breasts roughly through her bra. She arched her back, pressing her pelvis against his erection as they kissed deeply.

He was working his hand under the waistband of her jeans when Michelle's voice drifted up the stairs. "Evelyn? Your Aunt Janice is leaving."

Evie tore her mouth from his. "I'll be right there, Michelle."

She pushed away from him, straightening her clothes and wiping at her mouth. Without looking at him, she started down the hallway.

"Evelyn, wait." Thomas took her arm, but she shook herself free and ran down the stairs.

CHAPTER 10

"Hello, Thomas."

"Where are you, Evelyn?" Thomas sounded exasperated and annoyed even through her phone, and the childish part of her was pleased by his annoyance.

"Why?" she said.

"We're not finished talking about your trip to Europe."

"There's nothing else to say." She stared at herself in the mirror and adjusted her clothing.

"You didn't answer my calls last night," he said.

"I went to bed early. Fighting with Dad always tires me out," she said.

"Are you at home? I stopped by earlier, but you weren't there. Were you – were you at a bar?" Now, the annoyance had been replaced with anxiety.

"No, Thomas. I was not at a bar. And yes, I'm at home." She smoothed her hand over her round belly, smiling at herself in the mirror. She looked freaking amazing.

"I'm coming over," he said.

"Sorry, I'm just heading out."

"Where?"

She laughed. "Well, it's a Wednesday night, so the bar, obviously."

"Evelyn, stop messing with me," he said warningly.

"I'll stop by your place before I head to the bar. You'll have half an hour to convince me not to go to Europe."

She ended the call before he could say anything else and turned off her phone. She took a deep breath, shrugged into her coat, and belted it closed. She was really going to do this.

You shouldn't. He's just using you to satisfy a need. Are you honestly okay with that? It doesn't bother you to sneak around behind everyone's back just to be with him? You're not a teenager.

Yes, she decided, she was okay with it. Why shouldn't she have more of Thomas before she left? It would make leaving him easier, right? One weekend just wasn't enough. She deserved to be with him again, even if it turned out to be only for tonight.

Have some self-respect, for God's sake!

She silenced her inner voice with a viciousness that surprised her. She'd been in love with Thomas Sinclair since she was eight years old. If sneaking around was the only way she could be with him, then so be it. It was worth the hurt.

* * *

"Hey, Thomas."

Thomas sucked in his breath when he opened the door and saw Evelyn standing on the porch. Her blonde hair was sleek and shining in the moonlight, and her lips were stained bright red. The familiar scent of violets was carried to him on the cool breeze.

"Can I come in? It's a little chilly." She smiled at him and pulled her coat tighter around herself.

He stepped back, and she brushed past him. Her coat fell to just above her knees, and she wore black nylons and the same heels she'd worn at the bar that night. Jealousy surged through him. She hadn't been teasing him. She was going back to the bar to find someone to replace him.

She turned to face him and glanced at her watch. "The clock is ticking, Thomas."

Thomas closed the door, and she frowned at the look on his face. "What's wrong?"

"What bar are you going to, Evelyn?" he asked in a low voice.

She smiled. "I thought we were going to talk about my trip."

"What bar?"

"Why? Are you planning on showing up and dragging me out of there?"

"Yes." He didn't bother to lie.

She gave that low, throaty laugh of hers that drove him mad with need, and he curled his hands into fists as his cock hardened in his jeans.

"If we aren't talking about Europe, then I'm leaving. I have big plans for tonight."

"Evelyn, tell me what bar you're going to," he said.

"Nope." She shook her head and then paused. "But maybe you could give me your opinion on my outfit. It's new. I just bought it earlier tonight."

His gaze dropped to her hands as they pulled at the belt of her coat. She untied it, opened her jacket, and let it slither from her body to pool at her feet.

"Evie…" Her name exploded from his throat in a hoarse whisper.

"Do you like my new outfit, Thomas?"

He couldn't speak or move – hell, he couldn't breathe. She stood in front of him, wearing nothing but a red bra, matching panties, and black stockings. A garter held the stockings up, and her full breasts nearly overflowed out of the lacy red bra.

"Well?" She put her hands on her hips and tapped one high-heeled foot.

"I like it very much," he rasped.

"Good." She ran her hands down over her hips. "Thomas?"

"Yeah?"

"Are you going to just stand there, or will you take me to your bed?"

"My bed." He was picking her up before she could smile her approval.

He kissed her hard on the mouth as he carried her into his bedroom. She wrapped her legs around his waist and tangled her fingers in his hair, tugging the short strands. She kissed his neck, licking and biting as his fingers pressed deep into her waist.

"You smell good, Thomas." She bit his earlobe, and he gasped before dropping her on his bed. He unclipped her garter belt with trembling hands and grabbed her panties. He raked them down her legs and dropped them on the floor.

He knelt between her legs, pushed them apart, and buried his face into her sweet warmth. She cried out and arched up off the bed as he parted her wet lips and licked her clit. It swelled against his tongue, and he sucked hard on it, feeling it pulse and throb in his mouth.

She moaned his name and gripped his head, pushing his face deeper into her. Her thighs tightened around his head, her heels digging into his back, and he licked her clit with hard strokes as she cried out again and then climaxed with a shuddering cry of pleasure.

"Oh my God, Thomas. Oh my God," she repeatedly moaned as Thomas stood and shed his clothes. He snatched a condom from his bedside table and smoothed it on eagerly.

He was desperate to be inside of her, nearly bursting with his need to feel her smooth walls gripping his cock.

"Take off your bra, Evie," he rasped out.

She reached behind her and unhooked it, pulling it off and baring her breasts to his hot gaze.

"So beautiful," he said.

He knelt between her nylon-clad legs and leaned over her, taking one hard nipple into his mouth. He rolled it between his lips, sucking firmly on the sensitive tip as she arched under him.

Evelyn gasped and shuddered beneath him. Despite her earlier orgasm, her body was still on fire with need, and his hot mouth was driving her crazy. "Thomas, please." She grabbed his ass and tried to push him into her.

He rose to his knees and ran his hands up her shins to her knees. He pushed, parting her legs until she was wide open to him. He placed his cock at the entrance to her warm core and thrust into her. She groaned her approval and cupped her breasts, pulling lightly on her nipples.

He watched his cock disappear into her warmth and wetness and squeezed her legs hard, his fingers digging into her soft skin. She squeezed her pussy around him until he moaned her name. She reached between her legs and rubbed her clit with the tips of her fingers.

"Fuck, Evie, you have no idea how hot you are when you do that." Thomas groaned and looked up at the ceiling as he plunged in and out of her hot warmth. He wanted to stare at her, but if he kept watching the way her long fingers brushed against her clit, he'd lose control and climax.

Evelyn twisted and shuddered below him, her soft cries of pleasure growing steadily louder as her release drew close. He had to look, had to watch her coming apart around him, and he dropped his gaze to her soft body. She rubbed frantically at her clit, and he pumped harder in response. His balls

tightened, and as she arched her back and made a cry of pleasure, he plunged deep inside of her and shouted her name as
his orgasm roared through him.

Still shaking from the intensity of his climax, he pulled
out and removed the condom with trembling fingers. He
tossed it in the wastebasket and collapsed on his back beside
her. She patted his thigh weakly, and he gathered her into his
arms until she sprawled on top of him. She rested her cheek
against his chest, and he stroked her long hair.

"Thomas?"

"Yeah, Evie?"

"That was amazing."

He laughed and kissed her forehead. "That outfit was
amazing."

She snuggled into him. "I thought you might like it."

CARL RUBBED AT HIS CHEST. HE WAS AN EARLY RISER, BUT THE
growing tightness in his chest robbed him of sleep over the
last week or so. Being careful not to wake Michelle, he'd
slipped out of bed and quickly showered, hoping the heat
would help ease the tightness.

He stepped out on the porch and breathed deeply of the
early morning air. He stared at the sun peeking over the
horizon. He loved this time of the day. Others would be up
soon, but the ranch belonged to him for the next half hour
or so.

He stretched, rubbing at his chest again, and stepped off
the porch. He headed toward the barn. He would take Star
and go for a quick ride. He'd been under so much stress
lately that an early morning ride was exactly what he needed.

He glanced over at Thomas' place. There was a light in
the kitchen, even though it wasn't like Thomas to be up this

early. He hesitated and then changed course. He would ask Thomas if he wanted to ride with him. They hadn't spent much time together lately and would be spending even less time together in the coming months. Carl frowned a little. They should have told the kids last night, but thinking about it made his chest tighten even more and his pulse quicken.

Still rubbing his chest absentmindedly, he walked toward the small cabin.

* * *

"It's really early." Wearing just a t-shirt and boxers, Thomas joined Evelyn in the kitchen. He slid his arms around her waist and squeezed her tightly.

Evelyn took one last sip of coffee and tightened the belt on her coat. "I need to go home to shower and change into something more appropriate for work."

"I like what you're wearing." He nuzzled her neck, and she laughed and set her coffee cup down before twisting around.

"Yeah, but it'll be awkward if someone offers to take my coat."

He kissed her forehead. "Good point."

"Besides, I need to get out of here before everyone else wakes up." Her smile didn't quite reach her eyes.

"Evelyn, I'm sorry. I shouldn't -"

She put her hand over his mouth. "Don't apologize. I've changed my mind, Thomas. I came here last night to tell you I'm willing to keep this a secret."

"You've changed your mind? Why?"

She shrugged. "I like being with you. Plus, you're super good in bed, and I haven't been laid in three years."

When he didn't laugh, she ran her fingers over his cheek. "Don't look like that, Thomas. You're not forcing me to do anything I don't want to."

She kissed him and left the kitchen. He trailed after her and caught her just before she could open the door.

"Evelyn, I only want to keep it a secret because I'm worried about what your dad will think. He's been good to me, and I don't want to disappoint him."

"I know. You think my dad hasn't made it clear since I was little that he wishes I had been a boy? You're the son that Dad always wanted. If he finds out you're sleeping with me, he'll be disappointed in you."

Thomas frowned. Shit, he was fucking this up again. "No, that isn't what I meant. I mean that I don't want to hurt him. Not after everything he's done for me. If he finds out I'm sleeping with his baby girl, it'll – "

She squeezed his hand. "It's okay, Thomas. The truth is, I've been thinking a lot about what you said, and you're right. We should keep this a secret. Dad wants the best for *you*, and he'll never believe I'm good enough for you."

She smiled a little. "Dad's always been a bit of a fool."

"You're wrong, Evie. Your dad loves you. He's very proud of everything you've done, and he -"

Her smile turned into a laugh. "I do adore you, Thomas. You're so loyal to the people you love. I know Dad loves me, and I love him. But being proud of me and thinking I'm good enough for you? Not a chance."

"You have it all wrong, Evie," he said. "He's asked me so many times to watch out for you, to make sure you find the right guy to -"

She squeezed his hand again. "I have to go before someone sees me leaving. Come by my place later tonight, okay?" She opened the front door and smiled at him. "Kiss me goodbye, cowboy."

He kissed her, his hand threading through her long hair as he explored her mouth. She carried his scent on her skin, and a feeling of possessiveness washed over him. She did have it all wrong, and he would make her understand that tonight. Her dad wanted the best for *her*, and he would never believe Thomas deserved her.

Hell, *he* didn't think he deserved her, yet here she was, offering to play by his rules. He would do everything in his power to –

"Evie?"

Thomas tore his mouth from Evie's, and she spun around. His stomach dived straight to the floor, and he stared in stunned silence at Carl standing on the porch.

"Dad." Evelyn gave Thomas a look of dismay as her father backed down the steps of the small porch.

"I saw the light and thought I would ask Thomas if he wanted to go for a ride. I didn't realize he… that you were, uh…"

Evelyn hurried down the steps, stumbling in her high heels. "Dad, I can explain."

Carl's face was red, and he pulled at the collar of his shirt. "I need to sit down for a minute. Chest – can't breathe," he wheezed.

"Dad!" Evelyn rushed toward him as he staggered and fell to his knees. He sank to his side, and Evelyn knelt beside him.

She stared at Thomas, her face pale and her eyes swimming with tears. "Call 9-1-1! Hurry, Thomas!"

CHAPTER 11

Thomas paced anxiously in the waiting room of the hospital. The ambulance had taken Evelyn and Carl to the hospital, and he had quickly woken Michelle and driven her to the hospital. The nurse had allowed Michelle to join Evelyn in the emergency area, but Thomas had been forced to stay behind.

This was all his fucking fault. He knew he needed to stay away from Evelyn. He knew that if her father found out he would be upset. It had upset him all right. He'd had a damn heart attack on Thomas's front porch. If Carl died, if Evelyn lost her father, he would never forgive himself. His lust for Evelyn had overridden his common sense, and Carl had been the one to pay for it.

He scrubbed his hand against his face and wondered if he should ask the nurse behind the desk for information. Kneading his cowboy hat in one hand, he approached the nurse. Before he could speak, he heard Evelyn's soft voice.

"Thomas?"

He whirled around. Evelyn stood behind him. Her eyes

were swollen from crying, and she looked like she did that time a horse had kicked her.

"Is he…" He couldn't force the words out.

"He's okay," she said with a small smile.

He let his breath out in a hard rush, relief coursing through him. "Thank God."

She smiled again and moved to hug him. He stepped back, putting his hands up to block her. "Evelyn, no."

"Why?" she asked.

"Your father had a heart attack when he saw us together. What we're doing is so wrong. We can't -"

"He didn't -"

He spoke louder, drowning out her protest. "This was a mistake, Evelyn. I'll never forgive myself for what we've done."

"A mistake?" she said. "Is that all I am to you – a mistake? You think my dad had a heart attack because he saw us kissing on your porch?"

"I'm sorry. But yes, sleeping with you was a horrible mistake."

She stared at him, the raw pain in her eyes making his chest tighten until taking a deep breath was impossible.

"Daddy might not think I'm good enough for you, Thomas Sinclair, but even he wouldn't be so cold," Evelyn said.

He winced. "Evelyn, earlier, you agreed that we should keep it a secret. You said it was just lust and that you knew what we were doing would upset your dad."

She stared steadily at him. "I lied. You were right, Thomas. I am in love with you. I've been in love with you since I was eight years old. I'm sorry that I lied. I shouldn't have done that, but I knew it was the only way to be with you."

Her lower lip trembled, and she bit down hard on it

before pulling her shoulders back and looking him in the eye. "I know you don't love me, but I thought you cared for me a little."

"I do, Evie," he said. "I -"

"No, you don't. I'm a horrible mistake to you."

"That isn't what I meant."

"It doesn't matter anymore. You don't need to explain. I was a fool to think I could make you fall in love with me." She wiped away the tears caught in her lashes. "You should go home and take care of the ranch. Dad is doing fine."

"Can I...I'd like to see him for a few minutes."

Her voice was soft, but her words wounded him to the core. "Sorry, Thomas, only family members are allowed in the ICU."

* * *

EVELYN STARED AT HER CLASPED HANDS. SHE'D TAKEN AN UBER home and had a quick shower before changing her clothes. She had thrown the lingerie and the shoes and coat into the garbage. She wanted nothing that would remind her of Thomas Sinclair.

Once her dad had fully recovered, she was leaving for Europe. And when she returned, she'd quit the ranch and move as far away from this goddamn town as she could. If she were lucky, she might find a way to stay in Europe forever.

She listened to the steady beeping of her father's heart monitor as she stared at his lined face. It was early evening. After seeing how pale and drawn Michelle was, Evelyn had forced her to go home for a few hours' rest. Although she knew that her dad would be okay, worry for him still sat heavily in her chest. Did seeing her and Thomas like that really cause him so much anxiety?

Carl shifted in the hospital bed and opened his eyes. He stared at the hospital ceiling for a moment and then looked at Evie.

"Still here," he said with a grimace. He pushed a button, and there was a low whirring noise as the top half of the bed moved upward.

"You know you'll be here until tomorrow, Dad." Evelyn took his hand and squeezed it.

"Why? I'm fine. It was just an anxiety attack and bad indigestion. I don't need overnight monitoring."

"Better safe than sorry," Evie said.

He pouted like a little kid and then glanced at the empty chair beside her. "Where's Michelle?"

"She went home for a little while. She was exhausted. I told her I would stay with you."

"That's good. She needs her rest. So, you and Thomas, huh?" he said bluntly.

Evelyn flushed bright red. "Yeah."

"How long has this been going on? Were you – did you, uh, get together with him before you left for college?" He asked, his face going a little red too.

"No. Why would you think that?"

He laughed. "Evelyn Lorraine Crawford – you've been in love with Thomas Sinclair since you were a little girl. Everyone knows that."

She blushed again. "I tried before I left for college - he turned me down flat. And even when I returned from college, he was a perfect gentleman. It's only been in the last month or so that he, uh…"

Her cheeks were so hot they felt like they were on fire.

"Why did he suddenly change his mind?" Carl asked.

"I guess, uh, I mean…" she hesitated. She didn't feel like explaining to her father that she had gone to a bar looking for a night of meaningless sex and ended up seducing Thomas instead.

He suddenly held up his hand and laughed. "No, stop. I already know the answer to that question anyway."

"What do you mean?"

He rolled his eyes. "Thomas loves you, Evie. Linda and I have had a bet going for years about when you two would finally start dating."

As she stared at him wide-eyed and slack-jawed, he scratched at the top of his head. "Of course, both of us were way off. I said you'd be dating the minute you turned eighteen, and Linda said Thomas would wait until you returned from college."

"Dad, what the hell?"

He scowled. "I guess Linda technically wins the bet. He did wait until after you came back. Now I owe her five hundred bucks."

"You – you bet on your children?" Evelyn was pretty sure *she* was having an anxiety attack.

He laughed again. "Don't look at me like that, Evie. It was all in good fun. Linda and I have been rooting for you two kids for years."

"No – no, you haven't!" Evelyn forced herself to lower her voice when it rose to a pitch that could wake sleeping dogs. "You've told me for years that ranch hands were good-for-nothing asses, and I was to stay away from them. And you told Thomas to watch out for me, not to let me date anyone who worked a ranch. The two of you practically made me a nun!"

He held up his hands. "In my defense, Thomas isn't a ranch hand – he runs the whole damn place. And I asked Thomas to keep the others away from you because no one but him would ever be good enough for my baby girl."

"I – I – do you have any idea what… I mean…"

He frowned. "Spit it out, Evie."

"I've spent years – *years* – thinking I would never be good enough for you. Believing that you loved Thomas more than me because I was just a girl. He was the boy you always wanted. I kept my relationship with Thomas a secret because I thought you would be disappointed in him for choosing me."

"Evelyn! You are the most important person in my life. I love Thomas, but you're my baby, my little girl. I love you more than anything else in this world. I'm so proud of you, Evie. I'm proud of everything you've accomplished."

Evelyn sat back in the chair. Her ears rang, and her pulse thudded like a runaway horse.

Oblivious to just how deep her shock ran, Carl said, "Where is Thomas anyway? I expected him to be here, comforting you."

She stared at him. "Daddy, he…"

"He what?" He frowned at the look on her face.

"He was even more determined to keep our relationship a secret than I was. He was worried about what you would think if you knew we were sleeping together," she said.

"Oh, for God's sake!" Her father snapped.

Evelyn was actually a little happy to see his impatience. It meant he really did feel fine.

"Did either of you consider just asking me what I thought of it?" Carl said.

She shook her head.

"Well, you should have. You're both adults – I don't have the right to tell you what to do."

"You tell me what to do all the time!"

"I make gentle suggestions," her father said blithely. "Anyway, trying to keep you away from Thomas would be pointless. The heart wants what the heart wants, right?"

Her mouth dropped open again. Her father was not much

for romantic gestures or thoughts, and she wondered for a moment if his anxiety attack had brought on a near-death experience for him.

"Go on, Evie. Go to Thomas and tell him I approve." He smiled at her.

She closed her mouth with a snap as a wave of depression washed over her. "It's too late."

"What do you mean?"

"Dad – I – you had an anxiety attack when you saw us kissing. Thomas thinks you had a heart attack. He shut down when I tried to tell him you were fine. He said that what we were doing was wrong and that I was nothing but a horrible mistake he had made."

Tears flowed down her cheeks, and Carl reached out and took her hand tentatively. She took a deep breath. "You're wrong, Dad. Thomas Sinclair isn't in love with me. As soon as you feel better, I'll leave for my European trip. And then, I'm sorry, but I'm quitting my job at the ranch, and I'm moving away. I can't stay here."

"Honey." Carl squeezed her hand, and she looked up at him, sniffing loudly. "Seeing you and Thomas kissing did not give me an anxiety attack. Although," he frowned, "I don't like the idea of you and Thomas just shacking up. My little girl deserves better than that."

"Dad -"

He squeezed her hand, silencing her. "I had an anxiety attack because, well," he stopped and shifted nervously in the hospital bed.

"What?" Evelyn said.

"Michelle is pregnant."

"Holy shit. Aunt Janice was right."

"What?" Carl said.

"Nothing. Congratulations."

"You're not upset?" he said with an anxious look at her.

"Of course not. I'm happy for you."

"Michelle said you would be happy for us, and I didn't believe her. She wanted to tell you weeks ago, and I said no. I got myself all worked up about it, and I felt particularly awful this morning. I was surprised to see you at Thomas' place, but it didn't cause the anxiety attack."

She stared at her lap, and he tugged on her hand. "I'll talk with Thomas, honey. I'll explain to him what my anxiety attack was about."

"It's too late," she said. "I don't think I can forgive him for what he said."

"Evie, forgiveness is hard, but Thomas is worth forgiving. I promise," Carl said.

Michelle stuck her head around the curtain. "Hey, you two. What's going on?"

Evelyn stood. She wanted to go home, have a hot bath, and curl up in bed. She kissed her father's bristly cheek. "I have to go. I love you, Daddy."

"I love you too, Evie," he said.

Evelyn hugged Michelle hard. "Congratulations. I'm so happy for you."

"He told you!" Michelle said with noticeable relief. "I've wanted to tell you for weeks now, Evie."

Evelyn hugged her again. "You're going to be a great mom."

Michelle studied her. "What's wrong, honey?"

"Nothing that has to do with the baby, I promise you that," Evie said. "I can't wait to be a big sister."

She pushed past the curtain that was around her father's bed. "Call me if you need anything. I'll text you later."

CHAPTER 12

Thomas gulped down the rest of his cold coffee, jammed his hat on his head, and grabbed his truck keys from the table. He was going to the hospital to see Carl. He had spent a sleepless night staring at the ceiling and an entire morning pacing the house restlessly, and he couldn't stand it anymore. He didn't care what Evelyn said. He was family, and he had the right to see Carl.

He swung open the front door and staggered back when he saw Carl standing on the porch with his hand raised to knock.

"Carl? What the hell are you doing out of the hospital?" he asked.

"Well, I -"

"Christ! Get in here. You need to be sitting down." He took Carl's arm and led him toward the kitchen. He started to help him ease into the chair, and Carl shook him off impatiently.

"Jesus, Thomas. I'm not an invalid."

Thomas sat down across from him. "Why aren't you in the hospital? You had a heart attack yesterday, for God's sake.

Should you even be out of bed? Where's Michelle? Does she know about this? Does she know you're -"

"Thomas, enough," Carl said sharply.

Thomas shut his mouth with a snap and stared at Carl. Carl returned his stare. His gaze was a combination of exasperation and amusement. "I did not have a heart attack, Thomas."

"What?" Shock permeated Thomas's veins. "What do you mean you didn't have a heart attack? Evelyn said -"

"Evie tried to tell you what happened, but you were too busy breaking her heart to notice," Carl said.

His stomach twisted into a knot, and he stared at the table. "I'm sorry, Carl."

"I'm not the one you should be apologizing to."

"I swear to you I didn't mean to hurt her." Thomas continued to stare at his hands. He couldn't meet Carl's gaze. He couldn't bear to see the disappointment and anger in them.

"Look at me, Thomas." Carl's voice was low.

Telling himself to stop being such a fucking coward, Thomas raised his gaze to Carl's.

"Evie's been in love with you since she was a little girl. Don't pretend you didn't know that," Carl said.

"I know," Thomas said hoarsely. "I tried to stay away from her, Carl. I promise you I tried. But I…"

"You're in love with her too," Carl said.

Thomas stared at him cautiously, and Carl rolled his eyes.

"Don't look at me like that, Thomas. I am neither blind nor stupid."

Thomas flushed again, and Carl leaned forward. "I have something to say, and you need to listen closely. I've known for years how you and Evie felt about each other. Hell, it was written all over both of your faces. Linda and I thought the two of you would be together long before this. Christ, I lost five hundred bucks because I figured you'd pursue her when she turned eighteen."

"What?" Thomas had no idea what the hell Carl was talking about.

Carl shook his head impatiently. "It doesn't matter. What matters is that you tell Evie you love her."

"I don't get it. You have a heart attack when you see me kissing Evelyn, and now you want me to tell her how I feel?" Thomas said.

"I told you – I didn't have a heart attack. I had an anxiety attack." He held his hand up when Thomas opened his mouth.

"And the anxiety attack was not caused by seeing you and Evelyn kissing. Although I'll admit, it gave me one hell of a surprise. I didn't tell Evie this, but I figured the two of you would never get together. When she returned from college, and nothing happened, I assumed you'd both decided it wouldn't work."

Carl scratched at the stubble on his chin. "Anyway, I was surprised, but it didn't cause me to collapse. I had been feeling poorly for the last week or so."

"Why? What's going on?" Thomas asked.

"Michelle's pregnant."

"Holy shit."

"Yeah."

"Congratulations?" Thomas said.

Carl laughed. "Thank you. I was worried about Evie's reaction. She's been my baby girl for twenty-eight years, and I didn't know what would happen when she found out Michelle was having a baby."

He smiled a little. "I should have known she'd be happy for us. It seems so silly now to have been so worried."

"Carl, I thought you would be upset that I wanted Evelyn.

You told me repeatedly that you didn't want a ranch hand for her."

"I wanted someone who would love her and treat her well. That someone is you, Thomas," Carl said. "Besides, you're more than just a damn ranch hand, and you know it."

When Thomas didn't reply, Carl took his hand, squeezing it hard. "You're like a son to me, and I love you, Tommy. You know that, don't you?"

"Yeah," Thomas said as his throat burned, and he blinked back tears.

"Good." Carl cleared his throat roughly. "Now, go tell my baby girl how much you love her. You need to fix this, Thomas. Evie's planning on leaving the ranch for good. You'll lose her forever if you don't tell her how you feel."

"I hurt her badly. I told her what we did was a horrible mistake," Thomas said.

"I know. And trust me – Evie's madder than a wet hen at you. But she'll forgive you. I know she will. So, get your butt over there, beg for her forgiveness, and tell her you love her."

Carl stood and placed his hand on Thomas's shoulder, squeezing lightly. "It isn't too late to win her back, Thomas. And if you don't at least try, you'll regret it the rest of your life."

Thomas stood and hugged him. "I love you, Carl."

"I love you too, Tommy." Carl returned his hug and then pushed him toward the door. "Go on now."

* * *

EVELYN HAD JUST GOTTEN OUT OF THE SHOWER WHEN SHE heard the knock. Frowning, she belted her robe around her wet body and headed into the kitchen. She hadn't gone to work, instead opting to stay curled up in bed. A combination of stress and depression kept her in her bed, and she dreaded the visit to her father this evening. It would be almost impossible to avoid Thomas at the ranch.

She had finally dragged her ass out of bed with the thought that she would book her flight to Europe. Her father was fine. She could leave and not worry about him. She had a good amount of savings. If she budgeted carefully, she could stay in Europe for a few months before returning home.

Her inner frugalness cringed at the thought of spending her life savings on a trip to Europe, but she pushed it aside. Getting away from Thomas and keeping her sanity were more important.

She pulled aside the thin curtain that covered the small window in the door and peered out of it. Her pulse hit warp speed, and her stomach flip-flopped. "Go away, Thomas."

"Please let me in, Evie."

"No. Go away."

"I know where the key is, honey." He sounded almost apologetic as he showed her the key he'd taken from under the flower pot.

"I have the deadbolt." She glared at him through the window.

"I'll wait out here all day if I have to, Evie. You can't avoid me forever."

She bit her lip as she weighed her options. Part of her wanted to leave him standing on her doorstep like a lost puppy, but she knew how stubborn he was. He would sit there until she came out or let him in.

Sighing harshly, she opened the door and walked away as he closed the door gently behind him. She stood with her back to him, staring at the bed as she gnawed at her bottom lip.

"Evie, I'm -"

"Evelyn," she said.

"I'm sorry?"

"You don't get to call me Evie. That name is reserved for the people who love me. You can call me Evelyn."

"Evelyn, I'm so sorry. What I said was awful and untrue. Making love to you – being with you - wasn't a mistake. It's the best decision I've ever made," Thomas said.

Her heart was jackhammering against her ribs, but she stayed silent. When he reached out and touched her shoulder tentatively, she wanted to turn and throw herself into his arms. She hugged herself tightly and kept her gaze focused on the bed.

"I talked to Carl. He told me that he knew all along how we felt about each other. He said he was surprised it took this long. He said I needed to apologize to you."

"You always do what Dad tells you to, don't you, Thomas," she said as disappointment careened through her. "Well, you've done it. You've apologized to me. Please leave now."

"Evie – Evelyn, I'm not here because of your dad." He reached to caress the back of her neck, and this time, she started to pull away, her entire body trembling.

He wrapped his arms around her waist and pulled her against his chest. She tensed and stared straight ahead before tugging at his arms. "Let me go, Thomas. Please."

"I can't, Evie." He rested his chin on the top of her head. "I didn't come here because of your dad. I'm here because I love you."

"Stop it," she said. "Don't lie to me. You've hurt me badly enough."

"I'm not lying." He turned her in his arms and cupped her face, wiping tears from her cheeks. "I love you, Evie. I've loved you for as long as I can remember. I'm so sorry I hurt you the way I did."

She stared up at him, fresh tears spilling down her cheeks at the earnest truth in his voice.

"Please don't cry, Evie. If you give me a chance, I'll do

whatever it takes to earn your forgiveness for what I said," Thomas said.

Fuck, did she love this man. She couldn't deny it any longer, especially not when he was saying exactly what she'd always wanted him to say.

She grabbed his head, pulling his mouth down to hers. She kissed him hard, her tongue sweeping urgently between his lips. He cupped her head and returned her kiss. She could almost taste the relief in his kisses.

"I love you, Thomas," she said when he finally released her mouth.

"I love you too, Evie."

She pulled away from his embrace and walked toward the bed. Thomas reached for her. "Evie? What's wrong?"

"Nothing." She grinned at him as she untied the belt of her robe. "You said you would do whatever it takes, remember?"

She dropped the robe, and he inhaled sharply as he stared at her naked body.

"I remember," he rasped.

"Good." She reclined on the bed and parted her thighs as he moved eagerly toward her, yanking off his clothes hurriedly.

"You'd better get started then, Thomas. I have a few requests." She grinned up at him.

He cocked his eyebrow at her. "Requests?"

She cupped her breasts, her thumbs rubbing across her nipples. "More like demands, really."

He stretched out beside her, one large hand cupping her breast as he leaned in to kiss her. "I have a feeling this will be the sweetest apology I'll ever make."

"Apology?" She tugged on his head. "More like apologies, cowboy. *Repeated* apologies."

He grinned at her. "Whatever you say, ma'am."

EPILOGUE

"Is she still in labour?" Thomas skidded around the corner of the hallway as Carl looked up.

"Yes, she's still in labour." Carl's lined face looked grim, and Thomas's stomach dropped.

"What's wrong? Is it -"

"Nothing's wrong." Michelle walked down the hallway toward them. She handed the girl in her arms to Carl. "Here, take your daughter."

He kissed the little girl's cheek, and she grinned at him. "Hi, Daddy."

"Hello, Nina. How's my sweet baby girl?"

"Evie's gonna have her baby. Mama said so," she announced.

"I know." Carl kissed her cheek again.

"Hi Thomas, Evie's having the baby, and you almost missed it."

Thomas laughed shakily. "Yeah, I know, sweetheart."

He followed Michelle down the hall, smiling faintly when Nina said, "Daddy, can I have some ice cream while Evie's having her baby?"

He glanced back at Carl, who gave him a reassuring nod before smiling at Nina. "C'mon, sweet girl. Let's go to the cafeteria and see if they have ice cream while we wait for Evie to have her baby."

* * *

THOMAS STARED AT THE TINY BUNDLE IN EVIE'S ARMS. HE leaned forward and kissed his warm head before kissing Evie.

"I can't believe you almost missed the birth of your son." She smiled tiredly at him, and he kissed her forehead again.

"I'm sorry. I shouldn't have gone out of town."

She ran her finger across the smooth cheek of their son. "Actually, it's his fault for deciding to come two weeks early."

"He was impatient to see us," Thomas said.

She took Thomas' hand and traced the plain silver band on his ring finger. "I love you, Thomas Sinclair."

"I love you, Evelyn Sinclair." He raised her hand to his mouth and kissed it lightly as Michelle, Carl, and Nina stepped into the room.

"Hi, Evie," Nina said.

"Hi, honey. Come sit beside me and meet your nephew." Evelyn patted the side of the bed as Michelle hugged Thomas.

The little girl studied the baby carefully. "He's wrinkly like daddy."

Thomas snorted laughter, and Carl gave him a mock glare as Evelyn grinned at Nina. "He'll fill out in a couple of weeks and not be so wrinkly, honey."

The little girl leaned over and carefully brushed her lips across the baby's dark hair. "What's his name, Evie?"

"His name is Noah."

"I like that name." Nina kissed the baby again as Evelyn reached for Thomas's hand.

He squeezed it gently, and she smiled at him before looking down at the baby nestled in her arm. Thomas reached for him and carefully lifted the sleeping baby. He studied him, one large hand holding his head carefully and the other cradling his tiny body before sweeping his lips across the baby's forehead. Evelyn's heart swelled with love. She had spent twenty years waiting for Thomas Sinclair, and he had been worth the wait.

She reached for his hand and smiled at him. "I love you, Thomas."

"I love you too, Evie."

Keep reading for an excerpt from "Healing Gabriel".

HEALING GABRIEL EXCERPT

Morgan armed the sweat off her forehead and collapsed in the armchair. She was hot and sweaty, and her back hurt, but she was pleased with what she had accomplished. It was Saturday afternoon. She'd moved her meagre belongings into the carriage house this morning and spent the rest of the day cleaning the kitchen and removing the dust protectors from all of the furniture. Despite the breeze blowing through the open windows, it was hot and dirty work, and she sniffed her armpits. She would need to shower before going to the barbeque tonight.

She stood up and eyed the large couch. She decided it would look much better if she moved it to the other side of the room. She would move it and then have a quick shower.

She grabbed the arm of the couch and, with a loud grunt, pulled it across the room. It was even heavier than it looked, and she paused momentarily to catch her breath. There was a soft woof behind her.

The dog was back, and this time, it had brought a friend.

The second dog was another Australian shepherd that was smaller in size and grey and white instead of brown. The larger dog woofed again at her.

"Hi, puppy. Who's your friend? And how did you get in here?"

It woofed again and approached her slowly. It sniffed her jean-covered thigh, and she petted the side of its neck. The second dog approached, already wagging its tail, and she also gave it a quick pat. "Since you're here, why don't you two help a girl out and push on the other end of the couch."

The dog chuffed, and she patted its head and grabbed the arm of the couch again. "Move back, puppy."

With another loud grunt, she pulled on the couch. It moved, but she was beginning to doubt her ability to move it across the room.

"Jeez Louise," she muttered. "What the heck are the cushions stuffed with? Rocks?"

"What are you doing?"

She shrieked in surprise at Gabe's deep voice. She staggered back, tripped over her own feet and fell. The back of her head hit the old wooden floor with a hard thud, and she cried out.

"Shit! Are you okay?" The right side of Gabe's face appeared above her, and she groaned and rubbed the back of her head.

"Just fine." She held out her hand. "Can you help me up?"

He hesitated and then took her hand. He yanked hard, and Morgan, not expecting it, tripped over her feet again as she staggered upward and slammed into his hard body. He yelped in surprise and stumbled back, still holding her hand. The arm of the couch hit the back of his knees, and he fell backward, dragging Morgan with him. They landed on the couch in a tangle of limbs, curses and dust. There was a deafening crack, and Morgan shrieked as the bottom of the sofa dropped from under them.

The dogs were barking loudly, and Gabe shouted, "Vincent! Delilah! Enough!"

They quieted immediately, and Morgan, coughing from the dust, took stock of the situation. The seat supports of the couch had snapped under their combined weight, and she and Gabe were wedged together at the bottom of the sofa. Her lower body was caught between the couch and Gabe's hard hip, and her upper half was sprawled across his upper chest. She tried to push away from him and felt a sliver of panic when she couldn't budge.

She cranked her neck when the dog snuffled her hair and licked her cheek.

"Vincent, leave," Gabe growled.

The dog woofed softly and retreated.

Morgan gave Gabe a worried look. "I've broken your couch. I'm so sorry. I'll replace it."

* * *

The sound of Morgan's voice drew Vincent over again. As Morgan turned to look at the dog, Gabe studied her closely. Dust covered her, and a large smear of dirt was across her forehead. Her light brown hair was pulled into a ponytail, and she giggled as Vincent licked her forehead.

"Good boy, Vincent. Get help. Tell them Timmy fell down the well." She laughed again, and the corners of Gabe's mouth twitched.

She was pretty, he decided. Her eyes were blue like his, but light instead of dark, and she had tanned skin and a nice curvy body. That curvy body was currently lying snugly on his, and his groin was embarrassingly aware of it. He dropped his gaze to where her breasts pressed against his chest. She was wearing a t-shirt with a scoop neckline, and he could see a hint of her cleavage. It was enough to make the blood rush to his dick, and he thanked God that her lower half was wedged beside him and not on top of him.

"Mr. Dern?" He realized he was still staring at her chest and quickly lifted his gaze. She was studying him, and he automatically turned his face so the left side was pressed against the cushion under his head.

A small frown line appeared in the smooth patch of flesh between her eyes. He was struck with the ridiculous urge to touch it with his fingers and try to smooth it away. He cleared his throat. Her eyes were still on his face, but they weren't looking at the ruined landscape of the left side, nor did he see any pity in them.

"Mr. Dern?" she said again, a tinge of worry in her voice. "Are you hurt?"

"No, and call me Gabe."

"I'm so sorry about your couch. I'm a real klutz, and I -"

"It's fine. It was an old couch."

"Are you sure?" She bit at her bottom lip, and he almost groaned out loud. He had a full-blown erection now, and he was ashamed of his lack of self-control. He had to get away from her before she looked down and saw the tell-tale bulge in his jeans. His dick had a mind of its own.

Can you blame it? You haven't had a woman touch you in years. Hell, you've never even –

He silenced his inner voice bitterly as she shifted, her breasts rubbing against his chest. "Um, I think we're really trapped in here."

"I just need to move to my side. Hold on," he grunted. He twisted under her, worming his way onto his side, and she gave a small squeak as her head banged against the side of the couch.

They were face-to-face now, both of them lying on their

sides. Without thinking about it, he leaned forward, pressing against her and touching her head. "I'm sorry. Are you okay?"

"Yup. Stuff like this happens to me all the time. I'm a walking accident."

She laughed and moved her body experimentally. It made her pelvis rub against his, and Gabe could see the exact moment she realized he had an erection. Colour flooded her cheeks, and her pink lips pursed in surprise.

He groaned in embarrassment and pushed his way out of the couch. She hit her head again as he scrambled free, and he winced and took her arm, helping her out of the ruined remains of the sofa.

She dusted off her shirt, staring at the floor with pink cheeks. Gabe turned away and looked at the two dogs.

"I'm sorry," he rasped.

"It's fine." She cleared her throat.

His damn dick had finally decided to cooperate, and he turned back around, making sure to keep just the right side of his face in profile as he looked at her.

She was staring at the couch. "Gosh, I really am sorry about your couch. I shouldn't have tried to move it."

"It's not your fault. None of this would have happened if I hadn't scared you when I came in."

She cocked her head at him. "Why are you here anyway?"

"I came to see if the power was back on. I called yesterday to have it switched on."

"Oh. You know, I haven't even checked. Hit the light switch."

He flicked the switch by the door, and she smiled when the light came on. "Thanks for calling them."

"Yeah." He hesitated and then said, "The front door was wide open. We're a bit isolated in the country, but you should shut the door. There are coyotes and bears."

She frowned. "I'm sure I shut the door. Maybe it didn't latch properly."

"I'm sure you did shut it." Gabe eyed Vincent. "Were you being bad, Vincent?"

The dog ducked behind the couch, and Morgan gave Gabe a confused look. "I don't understand."

"Vincent knows how to open doors. If the door is unlocked, he can open the handle with his mouth."

"That's amazing!" Morgan clapped with delight as Vincent crowded up behind her. "You're the smartest puppy ever. Yes, you are, oh yes you are."

She crouched and petted the dog. Not to be ignored, Delilah nosed her way in. "Oh, you're a clever girl too, honey. Yes, you are."

Morgan kissed the top of Delilah's head as Vincent chuffed and head-butted her. She fell over with another loud thump, her elbow banging off the wooden floor. Gabe winced as Morgan popped to her feet, dusting her ass off with her hands.

"Whoops!" She rubbed vigorously at her elbow.

"Are you okay?"

"Yep." She glanced at her watch. "I should start getting ready for the barbeque, though. Did you want to drive in together?"

"I'm not going to the barbeque."

Morgan blinked at him. "Oh, I thought you were. Lacey said that you were going."

"She was wrong." He made a clicking noise with his tongue, and the two dogs followed him out of the living room.

ABOUT THE AUTHOR

Elizabeth Kelly was born and raised in Ontario, Canada. She moved west as a teenager and now lives in Alberta with her husband and a menagerie of pets. She firmly believes that a person can survive solely on sushi and coffee, and only her husband's mad cooking skills prevents her from proving that theory.

For more information about Elizabeth, check out her website at

www.elizabethkelly.ca

facebook.com/EKellyBooks

instagram.com/elizabethkelly_author

amazon.com/Elizabeth-Kelly/e/B00EOHZ0MS

bookbub.com/authors/elizabeth-kelly

ALSO BY ELIZABETH KELLY

Tempted Series

Tempted

Twice Tempted

Forever Tempted

Breathless

Tempted Trilogy (Books 1-3)

Red Moon Series

Red Moon

Red Moon Rising

Dark Moon

Alpha Moon

Pale Moon

The Recruit Series

The Recruit (Book One)

The Recruit (Book Two)

The Recruit (Book Three)

The Recruit (Book Four)

The Recruit (Book Five)

The Recruit (Book Six)

The Shifters Series

Willow and the Wolf (Book One)

Ava and the Bear (Book Two)

Katarina and the Bird (Book Three)

Porter's Mate (Book Four)

Bria and the Tiger (Book Five)

Rosalie Undone (Book Six)

The Dragon's Mate (Book Seven)

Rise of the Jaguar (Book Eight)

The Assassin and the Bear (Book Nine)

Elora and the Crow (Book Ten)

The Draax Series

Reign (Book One)

Rule (Book Two)

Rebel (Book Three)

Surrender (Book Four)

Survive (Book Five)

Salvation (Book Six)

Harmony Falls Series

Sweet Harmony (Book One)

Perfect Harmony (Book Two)

Forbidden Harmony (Book Three)

Redeeming Harmony (Book Four)

Absolute Harmony (Novella)

Beautiful Harmony (Book Five)

Reckless Harmony (Book Six)

Seasoned Romance Series

Bet Your Heart on Me (Book One)

Take a Chance on Me (Book Two)

Place Your Trust in Me (Book Three)

Individual Books

The Necessary Engagement

Amelia's Touch

The Rancher's Daughter

Healing Gabriel

The Contract

A Home for Lily

Saving Charlotte

Shameless

The Fairy Tales Collection

Broken

An Unlikely Seduction

Holiday Romance

The Christmas Wife

The Christmas Rescue

The Christmas Nanny

The Christmas Boss

Sordid Games